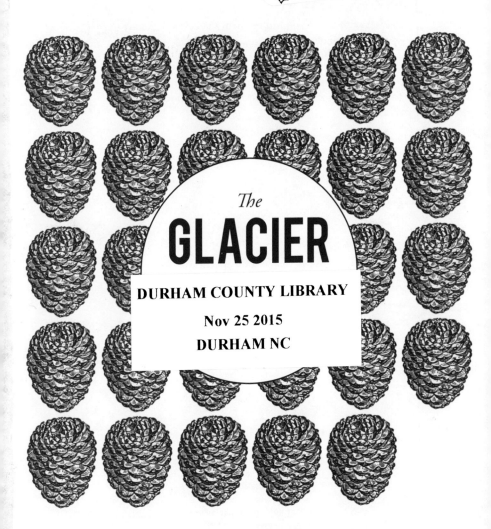

The

GLACIER

Two Dollar Radio

Books Too Loud To Ignore

TWO DOLLAR RADIO is a family-run outfit founded in 2005 with the mission to reaffirm the cultural and artistic spirit of the publishing industry.

We aim to do this by presenting bold works of literary merit, each book, individually and collectively, providing a sonic progression that we believe to be too loud to ignore.

Two Dollar Radio
Books too loud to Ignore

COLUMBUS, OHIO
For more information visit us here:
TwoDollarRadio.com

Copyright © 2015 by Jeff Wood
All rights reserved
ISBN: 978-1-937512-41-5
Library of Congress Control Number available upon request.

Cover: Cone of a pine, from *Elements of Geology*, The British Library
Page 3: The Great Serpent Mound, from *Ancient Monuments of the Mississippi Valley*, Smithsonian Institution Press, 1848
Page 98-99: Nelson Minar
Author photograph: Linda Rosa Saal
Design and layout: Two Dollar Radio

Printed in Canada

The
GLACIER

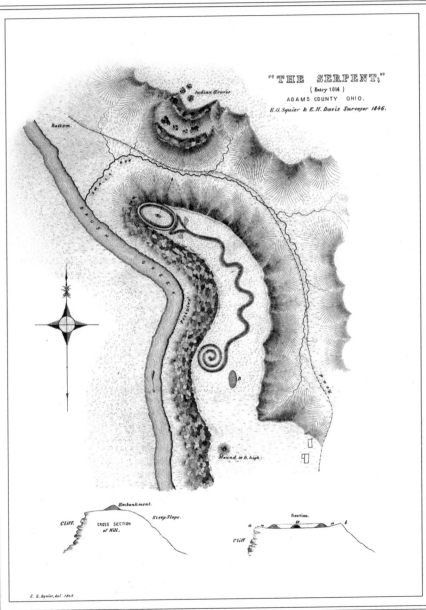

"THE SERPENT;"

(Entry 1014)

ADAMS COUNTY OHIO.

E. G. Squier & E. H. Davis Surveyor 1846.

Indian Graves

Bottom

BRUSH   CREEK

SMALL RUN

Precipice

B

Mound 10 ft. high.

Embankment.

Steep Slope.

CLIFF.

CROSS SECTION
of Hill.

Section.

Cliff.

E. G. Squier, del. 1846.

Lith. by Sarony & Major.

PROLOGUE
The Greening
An Aria of Trees

A stand of trees runs along the edge of a farm field. The spring trees and dense undergrowth form a panoramic still-life of green foliage, a familiar yet primal scene. A fracturing cradle of birds in the light. Slight hidden movements and chatter. Leaves and branches swaying, insects swarming the song, and just the greening, trees, alive.

‒ •••• •

A new suburban front door opens and a young boy exits the house in jeans and a jacket. He hops down the front steps, crosses the driveway in front of the garage and rounds the corner, heading up the narrow alley of lawn that separates his house from the neighboring house.

Beyond the odd space between houses, he stands at the edge of his backyard and faces a farm field that stretches out beyond. He looks out across the field and at the green stand of trees on the far side.

Rows and rows of low spring corn lie between him and the forest. An old lone tree rises from the center of the field, like a grandfather.

The boy's face.

Watching those trees, the fresh eyes of a seven-year-old boy. He looks over his shoulder at the houses and then he takes off. He sprints across the field, following a row of young corn toward the tree line. The brand new neighborhood of modest suburban homes sprawls along the edge of the field behind him.

.--. .-. --- -... .-.. . --

Maple, black ash, honeysuckle, and dogwood. A typical Midwestern forest. The trees are quiet, full of space, and intermittent bird-song.

The boy moves slowly through the undergrowth, alert, listening, and exploring. He runs his hands along the patterns of bark as he makes his way among the trees.

Treetops soar above him, spanning a canopy of filtered, emerald light. A woodpecker's tapping clarifies the cool air inside the woven cathedral.

The boy finds an enormous tree blown over in a windstorm. He stands before the massive root system, uprooted and exposed, marveling at the horrendous spectacle unearthed. He pulls himself up onto the horizontal trunk and eases along it as though traversing the keel of a capsized ship. He climbs through the branches of the toppled crown and emerges out of the top of the tree. Beyond it, he encounters a colony of wild grape vines. He holds on tight and in great running leaps, launches himself into Tarzan-swings across the forest floor. He takes up a fallen branch, as heavy as he can handle, to brandish like a broadsword. He swings it with all his might, smashing the branch against standing tree trunks, chunks and splinters sent flying through the undergrowth.

Deeper into the forest, the boy scrambles over marvelous collections of moss-covered boulders, rocky outcrops, and serpentine tree roots snarling over stones.

A small stream trickles into a gorge. Following it, he discovers a fantastic grotto many times his size. A thin glistening waterfall drops from a high ledge to a shallow pool on the cavern floor. He is a small figure, alone and entranced in this child's primeval wonderland—a seven-year-old boy, far from home, far from time.

.-- .. - ....

The boy descends the stream to a river. A broad river running through the trees. A row of milky, pealing sycamores on either side. Clear water flowing over polished stones and smooth, flat shale. High above the river, a colony of herons' nests are hung in the sycamores, a prehistoric enclave against the high blue sky.

He wades in shallow pools, negotiating the current over river rocks and from the safety of the bank he watches schools of minnows in sunlight plying over the ripples. He looks up from the water and is startled to see someone watching him from the opposite bank. A strange figure standing there, another child his size, but nearly naked and completely covered in pale mud paint from head to toe.

They stare at each other from opposite sides of the river. The boy cautiously stands and waves hello. The other boy waves back... a twin mirror image of himself, but covered in ghostly aboriginal paint. Then the primitive stranger takes off, disappearing into the trees.

‾.‾. .‾. .‾ ‾.‾. ‾.‾ .. ‾. ‾‾.

The boy sits at the kitchen table eating his breakfast alone, his spoon clanking on the bowl as he shovels down his cereal.

THE BOY
Can I go now?

MOM
Are you finished?

THE BOY
Yes.

MOM
All right, but you stick close by.

He flees the table, leaving his seat empty, his bowl and his spoon.

He explodes through the front door and follows his path toward the back of the house, sprinting down the alleyway between the two houses. He crosses the backyard and launches out across the cornfield.

The boy wastes no time returning to the stream. He moves steadily through the trees, sliding down a slope and descending to the water. When he gets to the river's edge he scans the opposite bank, looking for any sign of his strange new friend.

He sits down on a rock to wait. He waits and he waits. He releases broad sycamore leaves into the sweep of the current and watches puffy white clouds move across the sky above the trees. But the changing light brings a chill to the air and he huddles up on his rock, shivering. He scans the opposite bank of the river one last time but there is no sign of anyone. He heads back up the slope and disappears into the forest.

The boy moves through the trees once more, retracing his steps, heading home.

Emerging from the valley at the top of the rise, he suddenly hears voices and stops in his tracks. Adult voices. He hides behind a tree. When he peeks out from behind the trunk he sees them: Two men carrying some gear and pushing through the undergrowth.

Sue is holding a can of spray paint and tagging trees with orange paint as he moves along. He's running his mouth at Gunner, the man in front of him.

The boy watches them from behind his tree.

> SUE
> ...we've got good jobs. We get to work out-
> side, not in some sterile office. That's who we
> are. We're outside dogs. And I think it's kind of
> exciting. We're out here on the frontier, cutting
> trail. We're drawing the map and I think that's
> kind of neat—

Gunner stops abruptly and Sue crashes into him.

SUE

Whoa! Sorry...

Gunner holds up his hand to silence Sue.

SUE

What's the matter?

GUNNER

Quiet.

SUE

(whispering)

What? What is it?

GUNNER

Do you hear something?

The boy retreats behind his tree, listening.

SUE

No.

GUNNER

Do you smell something?

SUE

Like what?

GUNNER

Some funny smell.

SUE

I don't think so.

GUNNER

Well do you or don't you?

SUE

Well, I don't know! What kind of smell is it?

GUNNER

Something burning... It smells like something's burning.

Gunner moves on and Sue follows on after him.

The boy waits until they've gone.

He steps out from behind his tree and is startled to see another man standing nearby, watching him. The boy freezes and the man watches him quietly, with a friendly expression. Another surveyor, but a younger man, Jonah holds a long surveyor's rod in one hand like a futuristic forest staff. He takes a step forward, gently, but the boy retreats a step, scuffling in the leaves.

Jonah reaches a hand out, slowly, like he's trying to befriend an animal. The boy watches him. Then Jonah's radio suddenly squelches, obnoxiously shattering the quiet—and the boy takes off, disappearing into the trees.

‾ .... .

The boy sits at the kitchen table again, eating breakfast alone. He clanks his spoon against the cereal bowl.

He stops eating and scratches at his ear. He shakes his head and scratches at it some more. He takes another mouthful of cereal and then digs his finger into his ear, leaning over to the side almost all the way out of his chair.

                    MOM
            What's going on here?

                  THE BOY
            Something's in my ear.

Her hands on his head, and the boy's ear being examined by her fingers...

                    MOM
        Hold still, let me see. Oh—darn it. Leave it
        alone. I'll be right back. Don't touch it.

His mother releases him and leaves him for a moment.

Just the boy's ear.

                    MOM
            All right, hold still now. Don't move.

She steadies his head. Tweezers enter his ear and dig around inside his earlobe. He whines in a bit of pain.

                    MOM
            Eeew. Okay. Got it.

And she extracts a tick from his ear: a small deer tick, and still alive, its 8 legs cranking helplessly in the grip of the tweezers.

-.-. --- -.. .

The boy exits the house, closes the door, descends the steps, crosses the driveway, rounds the corner, and stops. Whatever he sees in the narrow passage between the two houses has stopped him in his tracks. He moves forward slowly, disappearing down the grass alleyway.

The boy stands in the grass at the end of his house, where the backyard would have led out into the field. Instead, there is a wall of beige vinyl siding, the back of another house.

He looks to his left and to his right. The field is gone. In its place is a long row of more houses. He looks up at the monolithic wall of vinyl siding towering above him where the view to another world used to be.

A lightly humming whir, air being moved through a ventilation system.

OHIO
WINTER 2000

A bare light bulb hangs from the ceiling of a self-storage unit. The bulb illuminates the small garage space of corrugated metal walls and a concrete floor. A large, obsolete word processor with a yellow-lit screen sits on a card table. A folding metal chair sits at the table.

Jonah lies on a mattress on the floor, his back propped up in the corner. He's in his 30s, medium build and fit, Midwestern decent looks. He wears brown winter construction coveralls, unzipped and peeled to the waist. The left sleeve of his thermal-underwear shirt is pushed up to the elbow and he holds this arm with his right hand as if he is wounded. On his left wrist he wears a watch. It is ticking. He shivers a bit, feverish, but he lies mostly motionless as if he can't move.

The quirky, tumbling music of an ice cream truck is faintly audible outside. He listens to it, breathing shallow, his breath steaming in the frigid air. He strains to check his ticking watch. Then he speaks to someone.

JONAH
Could you turn the light off?

A dark figure stands at the threshold to the garage space, silhou-etted and ringed by angelic halos from the vapor lights in the alley behind him. He moves forward and pulls the chain on the light bulb and Jonah disappears into darkness.

The harsh sound of the metal garage door rolling down and slamming to the ground.

.. ...

A momentary flash of a large tree on fire. The tree is burning ferociously in a dark winter field, roaring in the night, nothing but black around the burning tree and a ring of fiery light illu-minating the frozen ground.

‒ .... .‒ ‒

A vast, empty interior of smooth concrete and metallic light. An event hall after hours. On the far side of the hangar-sized room a steel door screeches open, throwing a long trapezoid of day-light out onto the floor. A figure enters and the door slams shut. Radiation Man walks across the concrete to the center of the space. He is an anonymous man wearing a radiation protection suit. He carries a hand-held Geiger counter.

He turns on the Geiger counter and takes a reading. The instru-ment chirps away steadily like a cockroach on speed. He turns off the instrument, walks back across the floor, and exits the room. The steel door slams shut behind him.

II

Ashen skies smolder on the black horizon. Rising light bleeds over skeletal treetops. Power lines cut across the countryside. Power transfer stations sit squatted in the weeds. Mutant cell phone towers rising out of nowhere.

Several morning deer venture out into the open. A buck scans the area, nostrils steaming in the cold air, a full rack of antlers balanced and poised.

Across the field, a row of suburban houses sprawls along the line between earth and civilization. A man's voice cuts across the landscape from an unseen walkie-talkie: the radio chatter of a land survey crew relaying abstract practical jargon intercut with static and squelch.

                    GUNNER
               (radio voice-over)
          All right. Good. Add ten. Good! Add five. And
          just a hair… Good. Shooting.

Brand new suburban houses. Thousands of new homes, everywhere for everyone. Condominiums, duplexes, and house after house, lined up like tombstones across the countryside.

GUNNER
(radio voice-over)
Got the shot. All right. And… Cut two! Good!
Let's shoot it again. All right, good. Shooting—

The white spray of a fountain aerating some half-frozen man-made pond. Wild winter geese camped out like refugees and wandering in the yellow, out-of-season grass.

GUNNER
(radio voice-over)
And— Got the shot!

Identical patterns of vinyl siding, milky windows, empty streets, and square lawns. The strange spaces between houses, strips of grass.

The new world is a brand new ghost town, and a cemetery.

‾ .... .

An automated suburban garage door opens, rolling up smoothly. The boy is revealed standing in the empty garage. He's outfitted for the cold in a blue winter snowsuit. But his cheeks are blazed with orange war paint. Orange and blue feathers rise from an "Indian" headband. At his side he carries a large orange tackle box.

He runs out of the garage, descends the driveway, and runs down the street, struggling with the tackle box that is almost too big for him to carry.

The little "Indian" boy wanders through the neighborhood. The streets are deserted, windows dark. He reaches a cul-de-sac and does a U-turn, walking a large circle around the perimeter of the dead-end. He sits down on the curb, fidgeting, alone, and gazing absently into the cul-de-sac.

Then he gets an idea. He walks into the center of the street and opens the tackle box. The box is filled with large sticks of colored street chalk. The boy chooses a color and draws on the pavement.

His stick of chalk goes around and around, scraping loudly against the street. He looks up and sees another child, a cowgirl, also about 7, snowsuit, holster, cowgirl hat.

> COWGIRL
> What are you doing?

> THE BOY
> Nothing… Making circles.

> COWGIRL
> I can do that too.

She grabs a stick of chalk out of his box and gets down on the ground to help him with his drawing. Around and around, the sound of chalk scraping circles on the pavement.

An outdoor labyrinth of corrugated garage doors. Rows and rows of storage units.

A single storage unit identical to all the rest. The door opens, rolling up with a manual clatter.

Jonah emerges from the garage. He wears his thermal construction coveralls, work boots, a winter hat, and a bright orange traffic safety vest.

He pulls the door down and locks it with a rotary dial combination pad lock. His breath steams in the morning cold. He pulls on his winter work gloves and walks down the long row of storage units.

.. ...

A middle-aged man sits on the edge of his bed. Pale, balding, and paunchy, Robert stares down at invisible stuff strewn across the industrial wall-to-wall carpeting. Only one side of the bed has been slept in.

The sound of a loud river rushes through the mundane suburban bedroom. The confusion of muddled dreams, sleep, and watery, groggy awakening. Robert pulls on his bathrobe and moves downstairs, leaving the invisible river rushing through an empty bedroom.

In the kitchen, he pours himself some coffee. Lite music and incoherent news voices interplay softly on the kitchen radio. He sits down at the kitchen table and sips at his coffee.

A ceiling fan rotates overhead, around and around, swooping loudly like the memory of a wartime helicopter in slow-mo.

Robert cradles the warm mug in his hands on his lap, looking down into the coffee.

.. ⁻.

A drive-in movie theatre screen watches over an abandoned lot. Weeds and small trees muscle up through the cracked concrete between rows and rows of old car-park speakers.

An all-white, very white unmarked ice cream truck is parked at the back of the lot by the concession stand, a small cinder block building.

Samson emerges from the building in an overcoat and mirrored sunglasses. He locks up and crosses the lot to his truck.

He cranks the ignition, turning it over several times before it catches and fires to life. He breathes into his cold hands, rubs them together, and waits for the engine to warm up. He's scruffy but handsome, with a huckster's jawline.

⁻.⁻. ⁻⁻⁻ ⁻.. . .⁻.⁻.⁻

A small corporate banquet room suitable for semi-intimate business luncheons. 10 round tables are covered in white tablecloths. Each table is set only with empty water glasses.

A young woman is alone in the room. Simone is in her mid-20s. She wears a cater-waiter's tuxedo uniform and is naturally pretty but pale beneath the fluorescent lighting and lite music floating down from the banquet room ceiling.

She moves from table to table, circling each table, filling glasses with ice water from translucent plastic pitchers. She moves with care and painstaking attention, not with the quick mechanization of a jaded veteran caterer, but as if a great effort were required just to be in the room in the first place.

Water and ice pour from pitcher to glass, clinking and singing like sensitive teeth.

⁻ .... .

Brown winter grasses sweep across the crotch of an exit ramp. Cars speed along the freeway in heavy streams of flowing traffic.

Jonah stands in the gravel along the side of the road, just a few short yards from the commuter cars whizzing by. He works with a land surveyor's prism rod, a metal staff about six feet tall. He holds the rod vertical to the ground as if he's planting a flag-pole. His walkie-talkie squawks—

> GUNNER
> (radio)
> Good. Got it. And... let's add 10 and we'll shoot 'er again.

Jonah un-plants the rod, turns, and walks in the gravel, counting out paces alongside the busy highway. His radio squawks again.

> GUNNER
> (radio)
> Stop. Good. Let's shoot it.

He plants the surveyor's rod in the gravel. He wraps his hands around the spirit level and eyes-up behind the prism. The prism is a golden mirror at the top of the rod used for reflecting a surveyor's laser.

> GUNNER
> (radio)
> Shooting...

Commuter traffic whips by Jonah as he holds the rod steady. The golden prism shimmers in some brief light.

> GUNNER
> (radio)
> Got the shot. Whoop, hang on. Something's
> funky here.

Jonah looks out across the gray suburban expanse. The rooftops of houses sprawl endlessly toward the horizon of gauze and ozone.

He pulls a small black notebook out of his back pocket and scribbles down some notes.

.--. .-. --- -... .-.. . --

Simone stops pouring water. She stares at the table, absorbed in some singular thought spread out across the white tablecloth.

The glasses on her tables begin to shake a little, ice clinking gently against cold glass.

.-- .. - ....

In his kitchen, Robert takes a couple sips at his coffee. He sets the cup down on the table and hesitates over something, preoccupied. Then he rises and leaves the room for a moment. The ceiling fan slowly stirs the room, eerily animating the empty space.

Robert returns with a double-barrel shotgun. He sits down and loads two shells into the 20-gauge. He lays the shotgun across his lap and sits stoically at the table, waiting and thinking.

He takes his pulse, feeling the loud rhythm of his own beating heart.

‾.‾. .‾. .‾ ‾.‾. ‾.‾ .. ‾. ‾‾.

The heartbeat is pounding.

On the side of the freeway, scribbling notes into his book, Jonah pauses and looks out across the city again. Traffic races behind him.

Strangely, all the cars slow down to a crawl and then stop. They begin honking impatiently until all the honking becomes a single stacked chord of overtones and undertones.

Then the honking suddenly stops.

In the eerie quiet, all the passengers are looking out their car windows in unison, like an audience at the theatre. Jonah turns and watches them all gazing out from inside their cars at something on the horizon.

- .... .

In the parking lot of the drive-in theatre, Samson's truck dies. He turns the key, cranking and grinding the starter but the engine won't catch.

-.-. --- -.. .

Robert turns the shotgun around and inserts the end of the barrel into his mouth. A piercing tone breaks across his kitchen radio.

.. ...

Out in the suburban street, the two children look up from their chalk drawing as a bright red cardinal passes quickly overhead.

- .... .- -

Alerted by something unseen, the herd of morning deer suddenly raise their heads from grazing.

- .... .

Jonah turns to face the horizon and quickly covers his face as a flash of blinding white light and a thunderous detonation emanate from somewhere out on the hyper-urban sprawl.

He lowers his hands to see a mushroom cloud forming above the rooftops in the distance.

.− −. ... .−− . .−.

From inside his truck, Samson looks up at the outdoor movie screen in disbelief.

A reflection of the mushroom cloud is exploding in broad daylight on the blank, white screen.

.. ...

The mushroom cloud soars and spirals over the low-slung skyline, a geyser of fire slowly unfurling like a proud peacock, ferocious and beautiful.

Jonah watches the spectacle.

The exploded cloud almost seems to hold its form, like a tactile sculpture, a cobra accumulating mass and power. Fire in the sky, dazzling colors of unearthly devastation above the monochrome metropolis.

And then it unleashes.

Looking down on the city, shock waves radiate in concentric circles from the center.

The city is overtaken by monstrous sound and fury as a wall of atomic fire rolls across the grid. Neighborhoods are annihilated by the shock wave. A sea of rooftops, fences, and vinyl siding is obliterated.

.. -.

Old-man Robert is blown away by a blistering atomic wind, the molecules of his body blurring colorfully into the drizzling wallpaper of his kitchen.

-.-. --- -.. . .-.-.-

Out in the winter field, the wild deer flash transparently, all skeleton and antlers, exterior shells disintegrating.

- .... .

The cowgirl and the Indian boy evaporate.

.--. .-. --- -... .-.. . --

The windshields of cars shatter like fine crystal as the shock wave rolls down the highway, an aria of glass exploding across the legion of commuter cars.

On the side of the road, Jonah watches the sonic wave rolling toward him.

And he is consumed—

                    JONAH
        Wait.

The Apocalypse pauses.

Jonah stands in a calm field of white light, a blinding brightness glistening and radiating between two worlds.

He searches in the luminescent fog like a blind man. Wide-eyed, looking at his hands and his body, a body of whirling molecules and orbiting atoms. Music, strange and gentle, soft bells and singing glasses. Beautiful, serene light—

—and then it's gone, fast, sucked out of the atmosphere, and Jonah is standing on the road, a charred skeleton.

Behind him, cars and bodies sit frozen, seared and smeared on the road, smoking like a Day of the Dead still life. Showers of shattered window glass hang in mid-air.

For a moment, the road is quiet and still.

Then the scene collapses. The windshields of commuter cars fall back into place like puzzle pieces.

Jonah's molecules reassemble, swirling into form.

And as though flowing toward some massive vacuum, the apocalyptic sequence reverses. Shock waves radiate back toward the center of the city and suburbia reconstructs itself.

.-- .. - ....

In the banquet room of the Convention Center, ice water flows in reverse, pouring up and backward into the pitcher in Simone's hand.

-.-. .-. .- -.-. -.- .. -. --.

The mushroom cloud implodes, retreating into its source. And in a flash of light the compression is complete.

Jonah clutches painfully at his left arm and looks around himself in shock at what may or may not have just happened.

A stream of commuter traffic flows smoothly behind him.

He looks out across the suburban expanse and his radio squawks.

> GUNNER
> (radio)
> Got the shot. Whoop, hang on. Something's
> funky here.

Up the road, a weathered Chevy Suburban is parked in the gravel with Jonah's work crew.

Gunner is a rounded bear of a man. A thick mustache hangs beneath a formidable snout on his red-cheeked and chinless face. He stands out in the cold behind the scope of a surveyor's laser gun mounted on a tripod.

Sue, on the other hand, is wiry, angular, and razor-clean. Easily chilled, he sits in the heated truck working out calculations with his engineering charts.

Separated by the truck window, the two men speak to each other with two-way radios even though they are only a few yards apart.

> SUE
> (radio)
> What's up, Gunner?

GUNNER
(radio)
Dunno. Hang on… There we go. Good to go.
Must've had a bug in the gun.

SUE
(radio)
All right, let's shoot the next one.

GUNNER
(radio)
Yeah. Good. Shooting.

-.-. --- -.. .

Robert has the end of the shotgun barrel in his mouth.

The radio whines a piercing tone.

RADIO VOICE
This is a test of the Emergency Broadcast
System. This is only a test. In the event of an
actual emergency—

Robert slowly backs off the shotgun, placing it gingerly on his
lap. He gets up and switches off the radio. He listens to the
silence in his kitchen. He looks up at the ceiling fan.

The fan is no longer spinning around.

Samson is grinding the ignition and racing the engine of the ice cream truck. Startled, he releases the key and takes his foot off the gas.

He sits back and allows the engine to settle, perplexed at the lost moment. He takes off his sunglasses and looks up at the blank movie screen. It is looming, but blank.

Then he throws a switch on the dash. A clumsy ice cream melody trips across the lot. Sam throws her into gear and pulls away.

- .... .- -

Robert steps out onto the back patio to get some air. He stands on the cold concrete pad, in his bathrobe and bare feet, shotgun at his side, gazing out across the frozen farm field. He spies the small herd of deer and the 12-point buck and watches them foraging at the ground.

Out in the field, the deer scatter at the booming of a shotgun blast.

- .... .

Simone is staring at the white tablecloth with a pitcher of ice water in her hand.

MR. STEVENS
Good morning, Simone.

Startled, she shrieks and spills a glass of water across the crisp new table setting. Standing across the room by the door is Mr. Stevens, a gaunt and imposing minister of a man in a tuxedo.

> SIMONE
> Darn it. Good morning.

> MR. STEVENS
> How we doing in here this morning?

> SIMONE
> Okay. Pretty good.

> MR. STEVENS
> Super.

He gives her a thumbs-up.

> MR. STEVENS
> Keep up the good work.

Mr. Stevens exits.

Simone catches her breath and looks back down at the wet tablecloth that now needs to be changed and reset.

.‾ ‾. ... .‾‾ . .‾.

Robert stands in his dull, dim living room with the shotgun at his side. The living room is perfectly ordered and composed, virtually unlived-in. He looks around the room, lost, as if he's unsure whose house this is, or what to do about it, as if he's never been here before.

He takes up a framed photograph from an end table and considers it impassively. He moves to the front window and peers through anemic, translucent curtains. He fingers the coarse, thin fabric and lets it drop, scanning the room for a familiar sign or indication.

.. ...

Samson pulls into a sprawling parking lot. He parks the truck, hops out, and crosses the lot toward the entrance to a mega-supermarket.

Inside the epic super-store is a colorful explosion of radiant products and packaging lined up like the codified end of evolution. 300 different kinds of cereal. Aisle after aisle of everything that you could ever need, for what's left of the entire family. There's a striking absence of elevator music. Oddly, the store is nearly deserted.

Sam pushes a shopping cart into the massive store, rattling the wheels from aisle to aisle, moving through the consumer paradise. He turns down an aisle and finds what he's looking for. He fills his cart with boxes of instant hot chocolate.

He turns to leave and then he sees something—

A mud man is standing at the end of the aisle, staring at him. The mud man is naked to the waist and covered in pale mud paint, like a ghostly aboriginal. The man also looks remarkably like Samson. The two stare at each other for a moment, like mirror images.

Sam turns and quickly pushes his cart down the aisle in the opposite direction. He walks back through the store, passing aisle after aisle. The mud man mirrors his steps, at the far end of each aisle. Sam watches him as they move together, spellbound by the strange and synchronous apparition.

Then he cuts into a checkout line and unloads the contents of his cart onto a conveyor belt.

III

A sledgehammer comes down hard onto a wooden stake, driving it several times into the cold, hard earth.

Jonah pulls off one of his gloves and places a small metal tack on top of the wooden stake.

His radio squawks.

> GUNNER
> (radio)
> Right just a little. Little more. All right, good.
> Let's shoot it there.

Jonah adjusts the tack as instructed and taps it into the top of the stake with his hammer. He pulls his glove back on and grabs the surveyor's prism rod. He places the spear-like tip of the rod onto the concave head of the metal tack and holds the rod level and steady.

GUNNER
(radio)
Shooting—

He waits, his breath steaming in the cold, both hands concentrated on the surveyor's staff.

GUNNER
(radio)
Got the shot. And— Good!

Jonah paces out a new distance, hiking over the hard-packed earth and counting out paces under his breath. The surveyors are at work, running a circuit out on a cold and bleak landscape. A large field has been razed for development. Nearby houses rise from the frozen mud and sprawl into the countryside.

Sue sits in the warm truck running numbers over his engineering charts with a pencil and an old calculator. Still separated by the truck window, Gunner and Sue communicate over their radios like astronauts on a lunar outpost.

GUNNER
(radio)
Okay, next set.

SUE
(radio)
Hang on. Gimme just a minute here.

Jonah pauses out on the field and considers the landscape about him, an arid enclave of brand new haunted houses, silent and brooding in broad daylight.

Gunner sips at some coffee and also observes the frames of houses in various stages of construction. Inanimate windows stare back at him, some empty and hollow, others darkened by new glass.

Sue works at his charts and numbers with pencil and calculator. Gunner interrupts him over the radio.

> GUNNER
> (radio)
> Sue.

> SUE
> (radio)
> Yes, Gunner.

> GUNNER
> (radio)
> You ever get uneasy out here?

> SUE
> (radio)
> Out here where?

Gunner shoots him a look and raises his voice, emphatically, not bothering to use the radio.

> GUNNER
> Here.

Sue rephrases, obligingly.

SUE
(radio)
How do you mean, Gunner.

GUNNER
(radio)
I mean where in the hell is everyone? For example.

SUE
(radio)
Who?

GUNNER
(radio)
All these fucking people.

SUE
(radio)
They're obviously not here yet.

GUNNER
(radio)
Either way, I don't know how in the hell they live like this. I'll tell you one thing, you unplug the mainline on these goddamn people and they wouldn't last two seconds out here all frantic and helpless like little poodle dogs.

SUE
(radio)
That'd be a sight, wouldn't it. Now just give me a second here.

Gunner kicks at the dirt and does his best to keep his mouth shut, his trigger-finger fiddling on the radio.

One window seems oddly placed on the side of a house, a single window on a wall of siding. A single dark eye.

Gunner lays back into the radio.

> GUNNER
> (radio)
> I just think it's pretty fucking weird that all of a sudden there's twice as many houses as there was five minutes ago.

> SUE
> (radio)
> All right, Gunner, let's cut the chatter. I need to concentrate for a minute.

> GUNNER
> (radio)
> But who are these people? What in the hell-God's-name do they all do?

> SUE
> (radio)
> They work, just like you and I do.

> GUNNER
> (radio)
> No they do not work just like I do. They breeze into their little cubicles in forty dollar socks and write little memos about which interstate gets to run through whose family farm.

Jonah scribbles notes into his notebook, overhearing their conversation on his radio.

                    SUE
              (radio)
     All right, Gunner, I get the point. Now shut it.

                    GUNNER
              (radio)
     No, you do not get the point. The point is
     that—

                    SUE
     That's enough!

Sue shouts from inside the truck, muffled like an angry bumble-bee in a glass jar.

Out in the field, Jonah looks up from his notebook—

And Gunner fires right back at Sue.

                    GUNNER
     Hey! I was from here! And I think I oughta
     know what I'm talking about. I was from here
     and now it's all one big fucking cemetery.

                    SUE
     I know where you were from! What I'm won-
     dering is if it's possible for you to keep your fat
     mouth shut for two fucking seconds!

Gunner moves aggressively toward the truck.

GUNNER

Well those are pretty big words coming out of
a little girl, mister.

Sue fumbles with his paperwork and locks the door just as
Gunner reaches out to grab the handle.

Gunner leans into the window and talks low, muffled and filtered by the truck window.

GUNNER

Sissy. You're always sitting in the truck with the
heat on. Why don't you come out here with the
elements and do a man's job for a change.

Gunner glares at Sue with wild animal eyes, steaming on the
glass with his snout like a bear on a tourist vehicle. Sue watches
Gunner, almost intimately, from behind the safety of the aquar-
ium. He parts his lips as if to say something but then stops
himself.

GUNNER

That's what I thought.

Gunner turns his bear ass around and walks away from the
truck. Sue gets in one last dig, calmly speaking over the distance
of the radio.

SUE
(radio)
Fuck off, Gunner.

Gunner turns and hurls his paper coffee cup at Sue. It explodes
coffee all over the truck window.

                              GUNNER
                    Church coffee!!

Sue looks out from inside the truck window, coffee running
down the glass.

Gunner goes back to the scope on the surveyor's gun and sights
up Jonah in the crosshairs. Jonah stands across the site, quietly
writing in his notebook. Gunner observes him and then speaks
to Sue over the radio again.

                              GUNNER
                         (radio)
                    What in the hell is this guy always writing
                    down?

But Jonah can hear him over the radio. He looks across the field
at Gunner, directly down the scope of the surveyor gun as if
they're looking eye to eye through a telescope.

Gunner pulls quickly away from the scope and snaps off his
radio.

                              GUNNER
                    Dammit.

He walks back over to the truck and speaks to Sue. From opposite sides of the window their conversation sounds muffled and
bubbled.

                              GUNNER
                    Roll down the window.

                    SUE
        Leave me alone, Gunner.

                  GUNNER
        I need to talk to you.

Sue thinks it over.

                    SUE
        All right, back away from the truck.

                  GUNNER
        Oh, come on.

                    SUE
        Go on. Back away.

                  GUNNER
        Jesus Christ.

                    SUE
        Well go on.

Gunner backs up a few steps. Sue cracks the window.

                  GUNNER
        What is he always writing down?

                    SUE
        Who?!

                  GUNNER
        Him.

Sue squints over his dash and across the field at Jonah.

                    SUE

I don't know. I never noticed.

                    GUNNER

Well I have. The guy never says shit and every
second he gets he's always writing something
down in that little notebook.

                    SUE

So what?

                    GUNNER

So I don't trust him, that's what.

                    SUE

Oh, will you quit being paranoid.

                    GUNNER

I'm not being paranoid. I'm observing is all,
and what I'm observing is one more thing I
don't need in my workday.

                    SUE

Gunner, we are not going to invent problems
where there aren't any, so just lighten up.

                    GUNNER

Now that is just exactly what they want us to
do. Just go along with the whole goddamn
thing.

                    SUE

What whole thing? What are you talking about?

Gunner looks back out at Jonah. Jonah gestures with his hands as if to ask, "What's going on?" Gunner looks over at the new houses, searching for an answer.

                    SUE
Can we get back to work now?

                 GUNNER
It's just something I think you should know about, that's all.

Sue rolls up his window and goes back to his numbers.

Gunner darkens...

                 GUNNER
            (ominously)
Suit yourself.

He lingers for a moment at the truck and then goes back to looking down the scope of the gun.

                    .. ‾.

A long pink corridor of concrete block and fluorescent tube lighting, frighteningly institutional and empty.

Around a corner at the far end of the hallway, the sound of a metal cart approaching, clanking and rattling through the industrial complex...

Simone rounds the corner, pushing a cart full of salt and pepper shakers vibrating on metal trays. She rolls down the long hall, attentive and focused, pink walls flowing by on either side.

Then an invading awareness sweeps across her face like a passing cloud, furrowing. She slows down and stops.

She looks at a couple of doors, unsure. She gazes down the long receding hallway, and back up the route she has just traveled.

She listens to the building, deathly quiet but for intermittent clanking off in the distance, as if there isn't another soul for miles.

She listens to herself, the invisible map inside her, of whatever country that is. She flexes her hands around the handlebar of the cart and looks down at the salt and pepper shakers gathered on the tray like a clutch of extraterrestrial spores.

Then she turns her cart around and pushes it back down the hallway, taking another turn and disappearing down another corridor.

-.-. --- -.. . .-.-.-

A clumsy, familiar melody in the air of the neighborhood. The invisible song floats down a quiet new street.

The ice cream man!

Samson rounds a corner and slowly navigates the glacial streets. Deserted sidewalks, lifeless windows, winter lawns, the strange empty spaces between houses— Somnambuland. The ache of a phantom limb. Out here the ice cream man is king. The truck brings a luminescent glow to the neighborhood, a white-hot cauter beneath the overcast.

Sam rounds another corner in the labyrinth, trolling for action. Suddenly a front door explodes open. Bingo!

A small boy wearing a silver snowsuit and a space helmet rockets out of the house. He sprints across his front lawn and launches out into the street. All engines, maximum warp speed. He chases Sam's truck down the center of the street.

Sam sees the boy in his side mirror and grins rakishly, watching the boy run... Then he pulls over.

The space boy looks up at Samson through his space helmet.

Samson beams down at him, radiant.

> SAMSON
> Hello there!

> SPACE BOY
> I'm in outer space.

> SAMSON
> You most certainly are! How may I assist your mission today?

> SPACE BOY
> It's cold.

> SAMSON
> Yes it is. But it can get very hot in outer space under certain circumstances like suns, supernovas, red dwarves, and Big Bangs. Then there's heat shield failure during reentry and

other misfortunes. You're familiar with all this,
of course.

Space boy is focused.

> SAMSON
> How about some hot chocolate?

> SPACE BOY
> Hot chocolate!

> SAMSON
> All right then. One hot chocolate coming right
> up… Here you are, sir.

Samson hands the boy a steaming cup of hot chocolate. Space
boy holds out some change in his little hands.

> SAMSON
> Oh, I'm sorry, but your currency is no good on
> this planet. Save it. No charge.

> SPACE BOY
> Thank you.

> SAMSON
> You bet.

A sickly woman emerges from a house and stands in the front
doorway in her bathrobe. Sam nods to her and she disappears
back inside, leaving the door ajar.

Sam climbs out of the back of his truck and walks up the front
walk with a doctor's house-call bag. He enters the house and

shuts the door behind him. The sullen beige house glooms in the flat midday light.

The woman is lying on the living room couch in her bathrobe and an afghan. She's looking into the daylight filtered through thin, gauzy curtains.

Sam enters and approaches the couch. He moves a box of Kleenex out of the way and sits down before her on the ottoman, obstructing her from view.

From behind the couch we see him speaking to her softly, backlit by the light coming through the curtains. We can't see his actions, or her, but we hear her quiet replies.

> SAMSON
> Is there anyone you would like me to contact
> for you?

> SICKLY WOMAN
> No. Just the bank.

> SAMSON
> I will certainly do that.

> SICKLY WOMAN
> Thank you, Sam.

> SAMSON
> You're going to feel a little prick here.

> SICKLY WOMAN
> Ah—

                    SAMSON
    It's okay.

                    SICKLY WOMAN
    Sam…

                    SAMSON
    It's okay.

                    SICKLY WOMAN
    Sa—

                    SAMSON
    It's okay.

Sam waits another quiet moment and then exits. Through the
pale veil of the living room curtains we see him take a real estate
lawn sign from out of his truck and put it up in the front lawn.

Sam fires up the melody maker and pulls away.

The sign on the front lawn reads: FOR SALE.

                    ⁻ .... .

Robert is curled up like a baby on top of the covers.

The dresser, the mirror, the night stand. A clock ticks over the
silence, surgically counting another day away.

A tiny, tempting melody creeps into the bedroom and dances
around his head like a swarm of drunken mosquitoes.

Robert opens his eyes.

He descends his driveway and waves Samson down. Sam pulls over and leans out the window like a thousand-watt bulb.

> SAMSON
>
> Howdy.

> ROBERT
>
> Hello.

> SAMSON
>
> What can I do for you?

> ROBERT
>
> Well... I'm not exactly sure.

> SAMSON
>
> Hot chocolate is pretty popular this season.

> ROBERT
>
> I'll bet. What else do you have?

> SAMSON
>
> What else are we in the market for?

> ROBERT
>
> I'm not sure. Something a little stronger, I guess.

Sam considers him.

> SAMSON
>
> You a cop?

> ROBERT
>
> No. Do I look like a cop?

SAMSON

Yes. Do I look like the ice cream man?

Sam opens up the rear of the truck and leads Robert inside.

ROBERT

Holy smokes.

The interior seems oddly and deceptively bigger than it could possibly be. Part laboratory, part showroom, the ice cream truck has been perceptibly re-sized and retrofitted as a state-of-the-art medicine wagon.

SAMSON

As you can see, I'm able to offer just about anything that you might be looking for. So. What is
it that you're looking for?

Hundreds of bottles and jars are beautifully displayed on glass shelves—a dazzling rainbow of pills, powders, capsules, and exotic plants.

ROBERT

Gosh. Something for pain, I suppose.

SAMSON

What type of pain?

ROBERT

A general sort of pain.

SAMSON

Physical or mental?

ROBERT

Well I guess it's sort of that gray area.

SAMSON

I see. Are you taking any medication, currently?

ROBERT

No, not really. Vitamins. Aspirin. Coffee, I guess. If that counts.

SAMSON

It depends on the quantity, of course. Can wreak havoc on the adrenals, but it's my weakness too.
How is your mortgage situation?

ROBERT

Fine. Paid off, actually. That's one thing I'm not worried about. Why?

SAMSON

Just a stress indicator.

ROBERT

What's this?

Inside a solitary medicine cabinet, behind a glass door, there is a vessel containing a silver metallic liquid.

SAMSON

Ah, that's just a novelty item.

ROBERT

It looks like mercury.

Robert leans into the glass to gaze upon the curious, attractive substance.

> ROBERT
> It's very beautiful.

> SAMSON
> Isn't it?

Sam moves to the work counter and begins working with a mortar and pestle and some herbal greenery.

But Robert can't take his eyes off the silver vessel. The shimmering liquid reflects a fish-eye view of the room.

> ROBERT
> Well, is it?

> SAMSON
> What?

> ROBERT
> Mercury.

> SAMSON
> Quicksilver, actually.

> ROBERT
> Oh… What's the difference?

> SAMSON
> Semantics.

> ROBERT
> What do you mean?

SAMSON

Exactly.

Robert draws a blank.

SAMSON

It depends on how you look at it.

ROBERT

Uh huh. What's it for?

SAMSON

It's not for anything.

ROBERT

Then why do you have it? What does it do?

SAMSON

It does have some therapeutic properties.

ROBERT

You just said it's not for anything. Mercury is poison.

SAMSON

Sort of. In a way, yes.

ROBERT

So you poison people?

SAMSON

Why would you say that?

ROBERT

Because that's what it is.

SAMSON
(more firmly)
Like I said, it depends on how you look at it.

The Quicksilver glimmers and glistens.

SAMSON
Many naturally occurring substances with poi-
sonous properties also have therapeutic uses.
This is called the law of similars, or, if you like,
homeopathy.

ROBERT
So what does it do, then?

SAMSON
It's different for everyone.

ROBERT
You're not answering my questions.

SAMSON
You, sir, are momentarily in my charge and this
substance does not concern you, except perhaps as an object of caution. Now I suggest
we focus on the issue at hand or terminate this
engagement.

ROBERT
I see. And what is the issue at hand?

SAMSON
Your condition.

ROBERT

Which is?

SAMSON

Chronic boredom. A pervading sense of uselessness. Loneliness, isolation, malaise. Textbook depression. Anxiety. General physical nervousness. Circadian inversion characterized diametrically by compulsive napping and insomnia. Regret. Remorse... Repressed anger resulting in self-deprecation, passive aggression—

ROBERT

All right, that's enough.

SAMSON

Denial.

ROBERT

Thank you.

SAMSON

Contempt. Bitterness.

ROBERT

Yes, I get the picture.

SAMSON

Impotence.

Robert glares at him, impotently.

SAMSON

Now what I would like to suggest is a very basic protocol—

ROBERT

I think I've had just about enough of your suggestions and amateur diagnoses. I don't believe you have any idea what you're talking about and I've half a mind to seek out a regulatory board or business bureau on behalf of the safety of the neighborhood.

Stand-off. Samson speaks calmly and confidently without a shred of doubt as to the accuracy of his knowledge.

SAMSON

The Quicksilver is a profound therapy in which the patient, having exhausted all other options, is injected with the element. Whereby, a neurological transaction occurs such that the benefit and the cost are relative, and terminal. The patient undergoes a complete psychological rehabilitation, the prognosis of which can, paradoxically, only be described as both highly personal and transcendentally impersonal. But in so achieving this level of catharsis, the patient trades his or her life.

ROBERT

That doesn't sound like a novelty item.

SAMSON

No. It's very special.

Robert considers this, briefly.

> ROBERT
>
> I'll take it.

> SAMSON
>
> I'm sorry?

> ROBERT
>
> You've sold me.

> SAMSON
>
> Oh, I apologize, but there's been a misunderstanding. The Quicksilver is not for sale.

> ROBERT
>
> But this is exactly what I'm looking for.

> SAMSON
>
> Yes, of course it is. It's what we're all looking for.

> ROBERT
>
> Then name your price.

> SAMSON
>
> Listen, I think this conversation is quite premature. Now why don't we take our time and think this over—

> ROBERT
>
> I don't have any more time. Look at me. I want the full deal while I still have a chance.

SAMSON

I am sorry.

ROBERT

But why?! I don't have anything to lose!

SAMSON

Because you don't deserve it! If you don't
have anything to lose, then you don't deserve
it. Now I recommend that you go back inside
your house and think about what you really
want for the remainder of your short time here
on earth before you mess around with irrevers-
ible consequences. Perhaps you may find that
you do indeed have something to lose.

Robert is speechless. Defeated.

Sam places a hand on his shoulder.

SAMSON

Listen. Let's start out with something reason-
able. On the house.

He offers Robert a nice fat joint.

SAMSON

Warm comfortable clothes. Nice hot cup of
ginger-lemon tea. Relaxing music. Some yard
work. And a long walk around the block. You'll
feel like a new man. Won't even recognize
yourself.

Robert takes the joint, cautiously.

> SAMSON
> And call this number. It may benefit you. Just
> make a reservation.

Sam hands Robert a black business card embossed with silver letters. It reads: *Event Horizon*.

Robert hesitates a moment longer.

> ROBERT
> (sheepishly)
> How do you know?

> SAMSON
> How do I know what?

> ROBERT
> If it kills you, then how do you know what it
> does? Before that, I mean.

Samson grins.

> SAMSON
> Now that would be something of a conun-
> drum, wouldn't it?

.--. .-. --- -... .-.. . --

The surveyor's Chevy Suburban travels down a cold country road on its way to the next job site.

Gunner drives. Sue rides shotgun and fusses with the radio, searching for a station. Jonah sits in the backseat, looking out the window at the passing countryside and making notes in his notebook.

Gunner adjusts his rearview mirror.

> GUNNER
> You sure don't say much, do you?

> SUE
> What?

> GUNNER
> Not you, Nancy. It's no wonder you don't have a girlfriend.

From the backseat, Jonah sees Gunner looking at him in the rearview mirror.

> JONAH
> What?

> GUNNER
> Are you guys deaf?

> SUE
> Leave him alone, Gunner.

> GUNNER
> I've noticed that you're always writing stuff down.

> JONAH
> Oh? Yeah, here and there. Just making some notes...

GUNNER
That's what I just said.

Gunner watches him in the mirror.

GUNNER
What are you writing?

JONAH
Aw, I don't know. Just thoughts, observations.
Poems. They're kind of difficult to explain.

GUNNER
That doesn't sound so difficult. Give it a shot.
We like poems, don't we, Sue? We're not com-
pletely stupid.

SUE
Yeah, sure. I mean, no.

JONAH
No, I didn't mean it like that. I'm just not sure
how to explain them.

GUNNER
Well why don't you read something for us?

SUE
Oh, Gunner, would you leave him alone.

GUNNER
I'm just making conversation.

SUE
Well, quit being an asshole.

> GUNNER

I'm not being an asshole. He said he writes things down. I'm just curious what he writes down.

> SUE

Did you ever think that maybe it's none of your business?

> GUNNER

If it were my business then I wouldn't have to ask about it.

> SUE

Well maybe if you weren't such an asshole to begin with—

Gunner slams on the brakes. Sue slams into the dash, spilling coffee all over the windshield as Jonah slams into the back of Sue's seat. The truck screeches to a halt in the middle of the road.

> GUNNER

There. Now I'm being an asshole. I wanna hear what he has to say. It's not gonna kill us, is it? Now read.

> JONAH
> But it's just, uh…

Jonah reluctantly flips through a few pages.

Gunner turns around in his seat.

GUNNER

I said read, goddammit. Read!

Jonah quickly chooses a passage and in his smooth Midwestern drawl, reads.

JONAH

—from a singularity on that line dividing silence from complexity. It came like a great tide, sweeping them away. A continual, invisible explosion of white heat particles twinkling and glittering in the ether between entropy and determination. Suspended and informed somehow, and brutally awake. A throbbing nerve node. Arced-mass breathing in the curvature of space as if released from its cage of flesh and skull in one precise flash. Titanium veins pounding with incandescent armies of nano-teleology. Bursting vessels of—

SUE

(cutting in, quickly)

Well I'd say that is a little different. No offense. Gunner, would you mind if we kept moving here?

GUNNER

Read some more.

Sue huffs and rolls his eyes. Jonah glances nervously between the two men and then continues.

JONAH

In the zone of twilight between the deep past

and the deep future, we are living our deaths and dreaming our lives. Across the ecstatic memory of the present how could it be otherwise? Hunt like a swallow in the last cavity of evening light because dusk is forgiveness and the fire in the tree is burning down heaven.

The men are quiet. The radio snows a soft flurry of static. Jonah shifts uncomfortably. Gunner gently switches off the radio.

He clears his throat.

> GUNNER
> Say that last part again.

> JONAH
> Um… the fire in the tree is burning down heaven. Beauty and cruelty are so close together that they can't see each other. For this we should be grateful that they are so close together. Death is laughing.

The truck is quiet.

Jonah reconsiders the last line—

> JONAH
> (to himself)
> Hmm.

—and makes a note in his book.

> GUNNER
> Get out of the truck.

SUE

What?

GUNNER

You heard me. Both of you get out of the truck. Now.

SUE

What the hell for?!

GUNNER

(fiercely)

Get out of the goddamn truck!

SUE

All right, all right! Criminy!

At a loss, Sue climbs out of the truck in a passive aggressive fit. Jonah follows.

SUE

Good lord, Gunner, what has got into you?

GUNNER

Move away. Over there.

SUE

Hell...

They move away from the vehicle and stand in the gravel on the side of the road, kicking at the cold stones. The truck idles.

Gunner sits in the driver's seat, staring down at some buried consideration. He looks up and through the windshield.

The road stretches out before him in a long line that eventually disappears into the trees. Just up the road a deer-crossing sign shifts slightly in the light breeze. A murder of crows shouts out across the winter field.

Gunner looks out the driver-side window, across the road, across the winter cornfield, and way out in the middle of the field, he sees himself, as a mud man, standing naked and covered in pale mud paint, staring back at himself.

> GUNNER
> All right, let's go.

Jonah and Sue hesitate, not so sure.

> GUNNER
> Well, come on.

They climb back into the truck and Gunner pulls away.

The fields beyond the road are empty, quiet, and still.

.-- .. - ....

A small storage room is filled with droning fluorescent lights. Thousands of salt and pepper shakers are lined up on metal shelves from floor to ceiling.

Simone stands at her cart, filling salt shakers with salt. The room is deathly quiet, so quiet that the sound of pouring salt is quite loud.

A flickering fluorescent light interrupts her and she stops to watch it. Then she returns to work. Salt pouring like sand through an hourglass.

-.-. .-. .- -.-. -.- .. -. --.

A country road runs through a stretch of trees.

The Chevy Suburban pulls over and parks on the side of the road. Jonah, Gunner, and Sue hop out and unload some gear from the back of the truck. The winter woods are naked and still. The men are pensive and quiet before the landscape.

Sue scopes out the area and then speaks.

> SUE
> All right, we're gonna run a line through these woods and out the other side. Gunner, we got an existing elevation somewhere so let's find that and set up here. Visibility shouldn't be too bad with the leaves down so you just head straight out in there about a ways and then give us a call.

> JONAH
> How far?

> SUE
> (irritably)
> I said about a ways. Couple hundred yards.

Jonah heads off into the woods with his surveyor's rod.

The trees are bare of leaves but the forest is thick with brown winter brambles and vines.

Jonah tramps through the undergrowth, blending in with the wintry foliage in his brown construction coveralls. He counts out paces under his breath, slowly ducking and weaving through the brush, pushing branches aside, stepping over downed trunks, and crunching across a layer of frozen fallen leaves.

When he reaches his count, he stops and slowly waves the red and white striped prism rod back and forth above his head. He speaks into the walkie-talkie.

                    JONAH
          You got me?

                    GUNNER
                (on the radio)
          Hang on. Yeah. Got you.

He drives his surveyor's rod into the ground.

                    GUNNER
                (on the radio)
          Shooting.

Jonah waits. The trees are quiet. He scans the forest. A woodpecker taps on a walnut tree.

He looks in another direction and is surprised to discover an animal very close to him, only a few yards away. A buck deer is lying quietly on the ground. Strangely, the buck is just watching him, either unafraid, or unable to move.

Jonah slowly walks away from the surveyor's rod stuck in the ground and approaches the deer. It struggles to its feet, wounded. A bullet wound leaks blood from its side.

Jonah carefully creeps toward the deer. He reaches out a hand. Closer...

And then his radio erupts with a burst of static—

                    GUNNER
                 (on the radio)
         All right, got the shot! Hang tight.

Jonah quickly silences the radio but the buck takes off, disappearing into the forest.

                    ‾ .... .

Robert pours himself a hot cup of tea and sits down at the kitchen table. He wears his favorite jogging suit.

He examines the joint that Samson gave him. His cup of tea steaming quietly on the table. He lights the joint with a match, and inhales, and coughs horrendously.

Then he relaxes a little and smokes some more. He sits back in his chair, smoking. He rubs his face and loosens up his neck muscles. He takes a sip of tea. And he smiles a funny little smile.

He examines the black and silver business card which reads *Event Horizon* and a phone number. He goes to the phone and dials the number. It's a brooding 1970s push-button wall phone.

ROBERT

Hello? Yes. I would, uh, I'd like to make a reservation, please. Uh huh. Robert Adams. Yes. Adams. Okay. Uh huh. All right. I see. Okay. Thank you. Goodbye.

He hangs up the phone and stands there for a second, lost in the face panel of the old phone. He lifts the phone off the receiver just an inch or so, floating it, listening to the dial tone. Then he floats it next to his head, listening to the dial tone arcing invisibly between the handset and his ear.

He holds his other hand up before the keypad and positions his fingers to dial. He slowly probes in the air with his fingers, searching like a spider for a number to dial.

But there is no one to call. He hangs up the phone and sits back down next to the kitchen table. He stares at the floor, at an odd angle, nursing a little paranoia, and settles back into the horrifyingly infinite quiet of the kitchen.

He remembers his tea and takes a sip, but he inadvertently snickers and almost forces tea out his nose. He snickers again, struggling not to spit out his tea when— CHIRBONK.

Robert hears a sudden sound at the window. He swallows his tea and listens attentively.

THUNK. FFFFLLLLLLLKUNK.

He goes to the kitchen window to have a look. BONK! Startled, he recoils as something hits the window. He looks again, cautiously. WHAM. Something is flying into the window.

He goes to another window. SLAM. THUNK.

Red birds are flying into his windows.

Robert crosses into the other room. He opens the curtains at the large window. Nothing. Then—

THUNK UNK UNK UNK UNK UNK UNK UNK...

The house is under assault. A storm of kamikaze cardinals. Hundreds of red birds hurl themselves into the windows.

Robert stumbles backward, falls over the couch and hides behind it, covering his head and ears.

THUNK UNK UNK UNK UNK UNK UNK UNK UNK UNK UNK UNK.

Then, like a bag of microwave popcorn...

THUNK.   THUNK UNK.   THUNK.

The storm stops.

Robert opens the front door and cautiously peeks outside. The coast seems to be clear. A dead cardinal is lying on the front steps. Then he sees the rest of them.

Looking down from above, the house is surrounded by a moat of red. Red birds are piled like roses, circling the house. The house sits inside a ring of red, a square inside a circle.

-.-. --- -.. .

Jonah moves quietly through the trees, deeper into the woods. He counts out paces and finds his next point. He shoves the surveyor's rod into the ground and jockeys with the radio.

JONAH

You got me?

GUNNER

(on the radio)

Hang on. Wave it around a little.

Jonah waves the surveyor's rod slowly back and forth.

GUNNER

(on the radio)

All right, got it. Let's shoot it.

He holds the rod steady.

GUNNER

(on the radio)

Shooting. All right. Got the shot. Coming to you.

Jonah releases the rod and waits. He has another look at the forest. Bare branches compose themselves in black fractal patterns against the sky. Roots crawl across the tapestry of earth and fallen leaves. Micro-canyons of bark and crisscrossed timbers. Evergreen needles.

He spies a pinecone lying on the ground. He picks it up and examines it. It's a nice one. Big and full and complete. He turns it in his fingers, admiring the perfectly irregular radial symmetry.

Suddenly the pinecone releases an electrical charge, shocking him, and he drops it.

.. ...

The fluorescent lights of the Convention Center flicker on and off over Simone's head in the small industrial room. She looks up from her salt and pepper shakers.

- .... .- -

Baffled, Jonah watches the pinecone lying inertly on the ground.

He picks it up again. The pinecone comes alive, pulsating with electric-blue light, like a bug-zapper. Now it has him with its current and he can't let go. He reaches out with his other hand and grabs the metal surveyor's rod stuck in the ground.

The entire forest around him comes alive, exploding with electric-blue light. Tendrils of electricity arc across roots in the ground, spiralling up the trunks of trees and then crowning. The current jumps from tree to tree until the entire canopy of branches is humming, buzzing, and crackling with radiant blue light.

- .... .

BZZZT— The lights go out completely and Simone is in the dark.

.‒ ‒. ... .‒‒ . .‒.

Gunner and Sue are tromping through the undergrowth, dodging brown branches and briars. Sue is marking trees with a can of orange spray paint.

> SUE
>
> Gunner, listen. I know this has been a hard time for you. I want you to know that I am truly sorry about the farm. I know how much of a blow it was and I know it isn't any easier considering the nature of the work we've been doing.

TSSSST. He marks another tree with paint.

> SUE
>
> But we've got good jobs. We get to work outside, not in some sterile office. That's who we are. We're outside dogs. And I think it's kind of exciting. We're out here on the frontier, cutting trail. We're drawing the map and I think that's kind of neat—

Gunner stops abruptly and Sue crashes into him.

> SUE
>
> Whoa! Sorry…

Gunner holds up his hand to silence Sue.

> SUE
>
> What's the matter?

GUNNER

Quiet.

SUE
(whispering)
What? What is it?

GUNNER
Do you hear something?

Sue listens.

SUE

No.

GUNNER
Do you smell anything?

SUE

Like what?

GUNNER

Some funny smell.

Sue smells, delicately probing the air with his nostrils.

SUE

I don't think so.

GUNNER

Well do you or don't you?

SUE

Well, I don't know! What kind of smell is it?

GUNNER
Something burning. It smells like something's
burning.

Gunner moves on and Sue follows on after him.

.. ...

Jonah stands at the center of the brilliant blue spectacle with one
hand on the surveyor's rod and his other hand unable to release
the pinecone. He quivers and shakes, conducting the massive
electric current as it contracts his muscles, fries his nerves, and
lights up the entire woods.

By the time Gunner and Sue arrive at Jonah, he's standing in
a funny position with the surveyor's rod in one hand and a
pinecone in the other. His eyes are rolled back up in his head.
Otherwise, the forest around them is calm and normal. They
watch him for a moment and exchange glances with each other.

GUNNER
What are you doing?

Jonah drops the pinecone.

From Jonah's perspective, the network of electric blue current
evaporates from the forest. He snaps out of it, startled and
dazed.

JONAH
Oh— Wow. What?

GUNNER
What were you doing?

GUNNER

Quiet.

SUE

(whispering)

What? What is it?

GUNNER

Do you hear something?

Sue listens.

SUE

No.

GUNNER

Do you smell anything?

SUE

Like what?

GUNNER

Some funny smell.

JONAH

Um. Nothing. I mean— Just having a look around.

GUNNER

Huh.

SUE

Well let's keep moving.

JONAH

Yeah. Yeah, let's keep moving.

Jonah grabs his surveyor's rod and takes off into the trees.

Sue watches after him, dubiously, and Gunner examines the pinecone.

.. ‾.

The fluorescent lights come back on in the salt and pepper room. Simone is standing at her cart of salt shakers. She looks up at the long bulbs.

She steps out into the hallway and looks in both directions. The long pink corridor is empty. A fluorescent light flickers way down at the end of the hallway.

She steps back into the room and returns to her work at the salt and pepper station.

MR. STEVENS

How we doing down here?

Simone nearly jumps out of her skin. Mr. Stevens is standing in the doorway. He holds a lit cigarette at his side.

> SIMONE
>
> Omigod you scared me. The lights went out.

> MR. STEVENS
>
> Yes, there seems to be some problem with the power.

> SIMONE
>
> Yeah… Um, how many of these are we going to need?

> MR. STEVENS
>
> I imagine we better hit all of them, just to be on the safe side.

> SIMONE
>
> Oh. Okay.

> MR. STEVENS
>
> Super. Thanks again. I know this isn't glamorous work.

> SIMONE
>
> Uh huh. Hey I was also getting a little curious.

> MR. STEVENS
>
> About what?

> SIMONE
>
> How long is it that we've been here?

MR. STEVENS
How do you mean?

SIMONE
How long have we— I'm sorry. I mean, today.
How long have I been working here. Today.

Stevens draws a blank on her.

MR. STEVENS
You know the rule, Simone.

SIMONE
Yes, I know, but where is everyone? Else.

MR. STEVENS
I'm not quite sure what you're getting at with
this line of questioning.

SIMONE
Do you mind if I ask you a personal question?

MR. STEVENS
I'd be delighted.

SIMONE
Do you have children?

MR. STEVENS
Of course not. We're all going to die. After all.

They stare at each other poker-faced and Mr. Stevens takes a
drag off his cigarette. The radio in the salt and pepper room
snows between stations.

SIMONE

Okay, well, actually I was wondering if I might
be able to take a short break today.

MR. STEVENS

You bet. Whatever you need to do.

Mr. Stevens abruptly checks his watch, causing Simone to jump
again—

MR. STEVENS

Well. Gotta run. Just hit as many of these as
you can. Thanks again.

Simone catches her breath.

−.−. −−− −.. . .−.−.−

The three surveyors are moving steadily through the quiet afternoon trees.

Gunner and Sue are tromping as a pair. Gunner hauls the tripod
slung over his shoulder. Sue carries his clipboard and can of
spray paint, occasionally pausing to mark significant trees.

Jonah hikes out ahead of them, moving through the bare winter forest, nimbly pushing branches aside, ducking and weaving
slowly through the brush.

Patches of snow here and there. Chickadees chattering and blue
jays caterwauling.

Robert is raking dead cardinals into a large red pile in the center of his front lawn. He claws at the grass with a leaf rake. He stops to wipe his brow and scans the neighborhood to see if anyone has noticed the odd manner of yard work.

The neighborhood is entirely empty and Robert is alone with his large pile of dead red birds.

.--. .-. --- -... .-.. . --

Jonah is standing in a small clearing in the trees. Before him lies a large mound of earth about waist high, rounded smooth and covered with healthy green grass.

Light shines through the sparse canopy, illuminating the mound of bright green grass, out of season amid the drab surroundings.

Gunner and Sue emerge from the trees behind Jonah and stand next to him at the odd land-feature. Gunner observes the mound for a moment and then takes off his hat in a gesture of solemnity.

Somehow taking the cue, Sue speaks in a quiet voice.

> SUE
>
> What is it?

> GUNNER
>
> Indians.

                    SUE
              (momentarily fascinated)
        Oh—

Sue hesitates, unsure how to proceed, shifting back and forth
uneasily. Jonah looks up at the light coming through the trees
while Gunner is fixated on the green mound.

Then Sue takes the cap off his can of spray paint. He shakes the
can, steps forward and quickly marks the mound of earth with
an orange X.

TSSSST— TSSSST.

Jonah and Gunner both shoot him an incredulous look.

                    SUE
              (defensively)
        What?

Spooked by his irreverence, the men look superstitiously back
down at the Indian burial mound.

                .-- .. - ....

Samson rolls through a sector of new streets on the fringes
of the housing development. A construction zone of exposed
foundations, housing frames, and dirt yards.

Cruising slowly, looking for signs of life, Sam spies a small ghost
standing inside one of the open skeletal houses—literally, it is
a young child wearing a white sheet with cut-out eye-holes gazing back at him. Then he sees another child, climbing up from
an open basement. Another dropping down from some rafters.

Another, running between two houses. And another, crossing the street in his rearview mirror. The children look quite young to be playing in a construction site.

But there are children everywhere! Coming out of the woodwork like rats.

A boy wearing a homemade superhero cape runs out ahead of Samson's truck. He sprints around a corner, his cape flying behind him, screaming a high-pitched alarm at the top of his lungs.

SUPER BOY
Ahhhh!!! He's coming!!!

Samson slowly follows the child around the corner. Little kids line up on the street curb, clapping and cheering.

At the end of the street a cul-de-sac reaches out into a field. The circular dead-end is filled with children coloring on the pavement with street chalk. Outfitted in winter gear—snowsuits, mismatched layers, and a hodgepodge of ragtag accessories—the kids are down on the pavement covering the street with colored chalk. Their little hands are moving furiously, gripping the large pieces of chalk in their fists, around and around, the sound of circling chalk creating a swooping, sweeping rhythm.

Samson pulls into a driveway, jumps out of his truck, and announces gloriously—

SAMSON
HOT CHOCOLATE!!!

The children cheer and surround him like a pack of wild dogs. Sam sets out a self-service thermos and some white Styrofoam cups. Then he wades through the children and walks across the cul-de-sac toward a house.

The skeleton frame of a house sits at the end of the street. The dirt lawn is filled with furniture. A couch, a recliner, coffee table, lamp, television. A family of contemporary Native Americans is bundled up and gathered in the front yard, watching TV.

Samson steps over the curb and up onto the dirt lawn.

An ancient woman relaxes in the easy chair in front of the television. She smokes a gentleman's pipe and when she sees Samson she regards him and motions to a small boy who takes off running into the house. Then she looks up into Samson's mirrored shades, gestures at him with her pipe, and speaks to him in Wyandot, an Iroquoian language.

A younger man in the family translates for Samson.

> WYANDOT TRANSLATOR
> She says that the Devil is a curious crow, and crafty too. Since he could not be God, he became God's mirror, and now we are not so sure who is who.

The boy emerges from the frame house and crosses the yard, struggling to carry a pair of gallon milk jugs. The jugs are filled with a bright Tang-orange liquid.

> WYANDOT TRANSLATOR
> But really it is easy. When we make a deal with

the Devil, we go to the Devil's paradise. And
the Devil is the only one who makes deals.

The boy places the jugs at Samson's feet. Sam pulls an envelope
of cash out of his coat pocket and hands it to the translator who
tucks it inside the blanket draped over his shoulders.

The old woman thanks Samson, smokes her pipe, and smiles.

> WYANDOT TRANSLATOR
> She says that the Big Scioto is frozen, but it's a
> good day for ice-fishing!

Out in the street, a child is scribbling furiously and methodically
with chalk on the concrete. Around and around his chalk goes…
Beyond him, many more children are scribbling in circles. The
sound of chalk circling on the concrete creates an overwhelming rhythmic, circling, scraping sound.

The entire street is ringed with children, drawing circles.

Pulling back and looking down on the cul-de-sac: incredibly,
the children have filled the entire cul-de-sac with colored chalk,
creating a circle-based drawing. Smaller dots form bigger dots,
which in turn form large circles. Hundreds of concentric circles resonate harmonically like colored raindrops on a concrete
pond.

The drawing resembles a giant aboriginal painting.

Pulling back even farther and ascending above the neighborhood, the street drawing continues. Unconsciously, the children
have created an image as the result of their collective circular

scribbling: a long green snake slithers down the street and into the neighborhood...

In the cul-de-sac, the snake's mouth opens around an orb of colored dots and circles as if it is consuming an Easter egg.

Ascending higher, the neighborhood is only a piece of a greater patchwork, a quilt of fields and suburban clusters. Ohio. The Great Lakes, and the Eastern Seaboard arcing across the turning planet. The Northern Hemisphere. Planet Earth hangs in the vacuum of black space. And the Sun, radiating fission, solar flares, swirling gaseous hurricanes, and light.

‾.‾. .‾. .‾ ‾.‾. ‾.‾ .. ‾. ‾‾.

Dust particulates floating in a stream of bright sunlight.

Sunlight on Simone's hands.

Simone stands at a large window on the upper mezzanine in the lobby of the Convention Center. She is a lone, organic figure within an otherwise cubist and off-worldly architecture. Golden afternoon light spills over her. She closes her eyes like a cat in the window, basking in the warm, much-needed sunlight.

‾ .... .

A gorgeous oak tree stands alone at the center of an empty winter cornfield. Bare black branches extend like gnarled fingers from the thick, centenary trunk of the tree.

Jonah, Gunner, and Sue emerge from the woods and stand at the edge of the field as though taking in a vista. They look out across the field, faces awash in the magic light of an early dusk. Sue breaches the moment.

> SUE
> All right, let's just set up somewhere here. We can tag this one and then get outta here.

> GUNNER
> What are they gonna build here?

> SUE
> Oh, I dunno... Let's see...

He flips back a couple pages of his clipboard.

> SUE
> *Event Horizon*... A Convention Center.

> GUNNER
> Huh.

Gunner continues watching the tree.

> SUE
> (to Jonah)
> Well you know what to do. Head on out there.
> (to Gunner)
> Gunner, let's see if we can get this in one shot. Then we can all go home.

Jonah starts off into the field.

Gunner then momentarily sees the tree and the entire field completely inverted and upside down.

GUNNER
(stopping Jonah)
Actually, I think I'd like to call it a day.

SUE
Just one more run. Then we'll call it.

GUNNER
Nah, it's getting cold and I'm hungry.

SUE
Me too but we're all the way out here and I'm
sure you got it in you to take one more shot.

GUNNER
Nope. I don't think so.

JONAH
I can do it, if we have to.

GUNNER
You stay where you are.

SUE
Oh come on, Gunner. Don't be ridiculous.
Help me out here.

GUNNER
I'm pretty sure I've made up my mind.

SUE
Don't make me pull rank here, Gunner.

GUNNER
Do what you have to do.

                    SUE
          Well then I will.

                    GUNNER
          I've got the keys to the truck.

Sue glares.

                    SUE
          Gunner, now I've just about reached the end
          of my rope with you. If you're not gonna take
          this shot then I'll pace out the distance and
          mark it myself.

He allows for a response but he gets none. He marches off
toward the tree with his can of surveyor's spray paint, counting
out the paces passive-aggressively.

Gunner's eyes turn wild and set and he calls out to Sue.

                    GUNNER
          I'm gonna have to ask you not to do that.

                    SUE
               (shouting over his shoulder)
          And if you leave me out here, then you can just
          forget it.

Gunner begins moving toward Sue as they shout at each other.

                    GUNNER
          Put the paint down, Sue.

                    SUE
          What is the goddamn matter with you?

                    GUNNER
        I said, put the paint can down.

Sue keeps walking.

                    GUNNER
        Sue!

Gunner runs at Sue. Sue takes off and Gunner chases him
across the field. He catches up and tackles Sue to the ground.
Sue struggles and kicks but he is no match for Gunner and
Gunner wrestles the can of spray paint away from him.

                    SUE
        Gunner?!?!

                    GUNNER
        I said, put the goddamn paint can down! Now
        how do you like it?!

Gunner holds him down and sprays orange paint all over him as
Sue tries to shield himself. Then Gunner sprays paint into the air
until the can is empty.

                    GUNNER
        It's time to go home and there's nothing we can
        do about it!

He hurls the empty paint can across the field and grabs Sue by
the collar, pulling him up close and eyeing his partner with ferocious intimacy.

                    GUNNER
        It's coming, Sue. It's coming.

Gunner drops him and walks away. Utterly bewildered, Sue watches him go.

Gunner marches aggressively toward Jonah. Jonah nervously steps aside as Gunner plows right by him, disappearing into the trees.

Out in the field, Sue gets on his feet, like a plucked chicken, ridiculously covered in orange paint.

The old lonely tree stands above him in the field.

-.-. --- -.. .

Gunner walks alone, methodically moving through the trees as if pulled by some force.

Somewhere off behind him, Jonah and Sue haul their gear, stomping through the underbrush. The forest is dimming and quiet but for the sounds of the men pushing through the branches and brambles.

Gunner speeds on ahead, urgently heading toward the truck, huffing, sniffing, and crashing, branches whipping at his face and thighs until he breaks out into a dead run and is running for his life.

.. ...

Simone is curled up on the mezzanine floor, asleep in the warm, diminishing pool of light. Curled up like a cat, dreaming.

Gunner is sprinting through the trees with complete terror-stricken abandon.

He careens down a slope, spills out of the woods, and stumbles into the middle of the road. He folds over and braces himself on his knees, panting and heaving, alone in the road.

Shortly, Jonah and Sue emerge from the trees, catching him in his moment of desperate recovery. They load up their gear while he stands in the center of the road catching his breath.

When they're finished loading, Jonah and Sue get into the truck and wait.

Gunner stands in the road looking at the truck for an odd extra minute. Then he climbs into the driver's seat, starts the truck, and drives away.

Gunner drives, Sue rides shotgun, Jonah sits in the backseat. The men are silent as the truck cruises down the wooded winter road.

Sue finally breaks the ice as they pass a deer-crossing sign.

> SUE
> Gunner. Well, I'm just sorry that things have
> come to this—

A deer suddenly leaps in front of the vehicle. Gunner slams on the brakes, but the truck hits the buck head-on. The deer flips onto the hood and careens toward the windshield—

Nothing but white light and a high-pitched chord, like wine glasses feeding back—

‾ .... .

Long banquet tables are covered in white tablecloths. Jonah is sitting alone at a table, hunched over his notebook, writing. He is wearing a cater-waiter's tuxedo uniform.

Simone is sitting a few tables away. She is looking at him. Oddly, both of their faces are covered in Kabuki-style white face paint.

Jonah looks up from his notebook and sees her—

.‾ ‾. ... .‾‾ . .‾.

The engine is idling. Thick, foul exhaust steams from the tail-pipe. The Chevy Suburban sits in the middle of the road.

Jonah stumbles out of the truck and staggers on the blacktop.

The prize buck is dead.

And so are Gunner and Sue. The buck is lying across the hood. Its head has gone through the driver-side of the windshield and pinned Gunner to the seat. His arms are hung up in the antlers and one eye has been gored. His jugular has been fatally lacerated.

Sue has been thrown over the dash and smashed through the passenger side of the windshield. His head is mounted like a wild boar on a wall of shattered glass, face splattered with orange paint, eyes wide to eternity.

A pool of blood runs across the hood of the vehicle and drips to the cold, cold road. Jonah wavers on his feet, absorbing the shock of the grotesque still-life. He manages to check his watch. It is still ticking.

Gunner suddenly spasms into a burning, primal grimace. He rages against the dead animal and the void, clenching its antlers in a terminal grapple. Then he surrenders, seeing it, and blasting out his last long breath like a blown steam valve. His foot slides off the brake pedal.

The truck rolls, creeping by Jonah like a ghost ship.

As the truck passes, a strange figure is revealed. A white mud man is standing on the other side of the road. Jonah gazes at the primitive apparition of himself.

The truck crawls down the road and rolls into the ditch.

Jonah is held in place, magnetized and paralyzed, fighting to run, but unable. There is nowhere to go, and he faces himself, the mud man, painfully, slowly collapsing. He sinks to the ground, brought to his knees.

The two figures sit on opposite sides of the road, gazing into the ghostly, mirrored images of each other.

Jonah quivers and shakes, fighting something mean.

Blood running from their noses.

Staring it down.

IV

The sun goes down on the Ohio countryside.

Bare winter cornfields are ablaze in the magic light of dusk. Flocks of black crows shout across the fields. Black treetops silhouette against the horizon-sky.

Remote radio towers, high-tension power lines, and drifting streams of jet-wash cut across the atmosphere swirling in cobalt and lava.

Robert takes an evening walk, alone on the sidewalks. Streetlights are fading on, but the houses are dark. Yards and streets deserted. Driveways empty. Windows blank.

He crosses a street and turns a corner. He walks an arc along the perfect curve of a curb. Is someone following him? Is someone watching from inside these gloomy windows? No, probably not. Not even from the strange spaces between the houses, or from the black trees beyond. Robert is alone at the center of the hive.

He stops in the middle of an intersection and waits for a car to come. Nothing. Does anyone else live here? He waits, scanning the neighborhood from the center of the street. No motion at all.

The world is in a coma.

.. ...

The monstrous Main Hall of the Convention Center careens with space like the interior of an enormous insect carcass. The hall is filled with round tables covered with white tablecloths. 500 white-clothed tables lying in wait like a field of eggs in an off-world hatchery.

A door opens on the far side and Simone enters the room pushing a metal cart full of clanking silverware. She makes her way across the space. Alone, she is a singular form crossing a lunar landscape.

She pushes her cart to the center of the room. She pulls on a pair of soft white polishing mitts and begins setting the tables. A simple yet monumental task, she shines dinner knives with a dish rag and sets them in their proper place at each table. 500 tables. 10 chairs per table. 5000 dinner knives.

Each shiny knife goes just so. A place for every knife, every knife in its place. Simone completes a table and moves on to the next. But she is surprised to find that the next table has already been set.

Unable to explain this, she ponders the table arranged with glistening silver knives, and wonders if she has misplaced a memory in the sequence. She runs a finger along the arced edge of the table.

She looks over her shoulder and up the long row of tables that she had been following. She scans the giant room, looking to see if anyone else has been helping her and she calls out across the hall.

                    SIMONE
      Hello?

From the far perimeter of the room, Simone is just a tiny figure in a sea of white tables, alone in the great hall.

But a small childlike voice replies.

                    SIMONE
      Hi.

                    .. ‾.

The light is almost gone. An incomplete street-stub extends out into a field beyond the houses.

Robert approaches the dead-end and stands in the glow of the last streetlight. He gazes out into the field. The black field, beyond the ring of light. Beyond civilization. He shudders against the cold, alone, looking into the question stretched out before him.

He steps out over the end of the street and stands in the dirt at the perimeter of visibility. He reaches out, extending his arm into the black night, probing to touch the void with his fingers.

His hand disappears entirely in the black and then he quickly withdraws it, caressing it to make sure that it's still there.

Robert cautiously takes a step forward, moving closer to the black void. He leans into it, peering, courageously for a moment, the front side of his upper torso disappearing—

He withdraws with a gasp and stumbles backward. Then he turns his back on it and walks quickly into the safety of the neighborhood.

-.-. --- -.. . .-.-.-

Back in the Convention Center the sound of silverware clinks through the great hall like tiny steel bells. As we move like a satellite around the perimeter of the enormous room, Simone is a small figure at the center of it. And her voice.

> SIMONE
> No, it's okay. It's easy. See? Just like this. A knife goes down on the table, pointed toward the center, perpendicular to the edge. Oh, you're welcome. It's nice to meet you too. Really? I'm sorry, I don't remember. Oh? That's funny—

She stops, quiet for a moment, at the far center of the room.

She places her hand on the white tablecloth.

> SIMONE
> Well, I should probably— No, I'm not going anywhere. There's just a lot to do here. Yes, an Event.

No. That's horrible... Why would you say something like that? I think we should stop talking now. I told you why. I know, it is kind of silly but that's the way it is. I don't want it to be that way either but there isn't anything I can do about it. Oh thank you but I don't think there's any way you can help. I'd love to but I can't right now. No. Thank you. Yes, of course. No, I don't want you to be sad but I do think we should stop talking now because I have to keep working. No, I don't want you to be mad either. No, I just— I think you should go away now. No! Stop it. No—

Simone explodes with rage.

                    SIMONE
          I said STOP IT!

Her scream detonates across the massive hall like a bullet puncturing a steel drum—

                    ⁻ .... .

In an empty white breakroom, a group of cater-waiters in tuxedo uniforms are sitting in banquet chairs arranged around an empty center. They are listening to free jazz very loudly. Their faces are all painted white.

After a stretched moment of deafening modal horns, bass, piano, and percussion, one of the waiters stands up and turns his head toward the camera—

.--. .-. --- -... .-.. . --

Suddenly back in the Main Hall, Simone lifts her hand off the white tablecloth. She turns around and sees that she is not alone. The hall is filled with co-workers, other servers in tuxedos, setting the tables.

They are all looking at her.

Then in unison they return to work and the hall fills with the sound of clinking silverware falling like a metal waterfall.

Simone stands motionless at her table. She slowly places a knife down on the tablecloth. She tries to continue, but then she sets all her knives down and quickly walks across the hall toward the exit.

.-- .. - ....

Robert walks back down the street toward his house. When he arrives at his driveway he notices that his porch light is the only sign of life in the neighborhood.

                    ROBERT
          Hello!

He shouts and receives no answer.

                    ROBERT
          Anybody home?!

No response.

Curious now, Robert approaches the house across the street. He knocks on the front door and rings the doorbell. Seems nobody's home. He tries the doorknob and to his surprise it opens. He steps back, cautiously, and lets the door swing open.

He peers in a bit and then steps inside.

The strange house is dim and apparently vacant.

> ROBERT
> Hello? Anybody home?

He finds a light switch. A bare bulb on the ceiling reveals that the house is not so strange. It's exactly like his own, except completely empty. No one has moved in yet.

Robert cautiously explores the house. He checks out the kitchen and runs water in the sink. He pokes his head into the garage. He opens the door to the basement and descends halfway into the darkness before he stops and scurries back up the stairs, boyish fear snapping at his heels.

He goes upstairs and walks down the hall. He opens the doors to a few bedrooms and checks out the bathroom. Shower with no curtain. Empty mirrored medicine cabinet.

Robert enters the last bedroom and turns on the light. A naked white mud man is standing in the corner of the empty room.

> MUD MAN
> Hello.

Shock accelerating from the base of his being, Robert frantically claws his way out of the room, through the hall and down the stairs.

He spills out of the house, sprinting across the lawn and street, ascending his driveway, fumbling with the key in the lock, and slamming the front door.

Inside the safety of his own house, he heaves himself against the front door, his own hyperventilating mass preventing all evils from entering.

The doorbell rings, a classic two-tone. Robert clamps down, full stop, all nerves, listening.

The bell rings again.

He steps away from the door, as quietly as he can, facing it and contemplating the other side. The doorbell rings a third time and almost out of annoyed bravado Robert flings the door open—

The mud man stands on his doorstep.

MUD MAN

Hello—

—and Robert slams the door shut, almost all in one motion.

He goes to the hall closest, leaving the front door unattended, and he returns with his shotgun. He flings the door open and stands back with the long-arm pointed at the ghostly visitor. Then he realizes that he's pointing his gun at a vision of himself.

Bewildered, he slowly lowers the gun. The mud man walks past Robert and enters the house. Robert stands aside and watches him.

The mud man looks around the house. He disappears into the kitchen and then returns. He goes to the curtain and fingers the texture of the fabric.

He goes to the table next to Robert's chair and picks up a picture frame. With his back to Robert he takes his time looking into the picture.

> ROBERT
> Who are you?

> MUD MAN
> I am the future of the past.

He sits down in Robert's chair and stares at the dark TV.

> ROBERT
> I don't understand.

> MUD MAN
> Then I will show you.

The mud man gets up and goes to Robert and takes the shotgun from Robert's hands. He turns the shotgun around and, squatting like a Samurai, places the end of the barrel in his mouth. He looks at Robert and pulls the trigger, blasting his own brains out the back of his head.

Robert winces, horrified.

But the mud man is still looking at him.

MUD MAN

There is no ghost in the machine.

The mud man drops the shotgun and collapses into a heap on the living room floor. For a moment, Robert watches the corpse in disbelief. Then he stumbles out the front door.

He stands on the lawn, shouting.

ROBERT
Help! Help me! Please, somebody help me!

There is no response from the neighborhood. Robert falls to his knees, retching and then sobbing.

ROBERT
Oh, I'm so sorry. I miss you.
I miss you so much. Please help me.

He sits down in the grass and cries like a baby.

The neighborhood is quiet, almost peaceful. Robert notices that a corner of sod is sticking up from the lawn. He crawls over to the offending piece of lawn and pushes the corner of grass back down into place.

Then he pulls it up again. He pushes it back down. He gets up on his knees and pulls away the entire section of sod, leaving a square of dirt exposed in the lawn.

Robert carries the section of sod into his house.

In the parking lot of the drive-in movie theatre, a car-park speaker hangs from its pole like the sullen face of a retired android. But it's croaking rhythmically, like a bullfrog. Another one peeps like a tiny tree frog, and another chirping like a cricket.

On the outdoor movie screen luminescent green organisms quiver and wriggle in a primordial fluid, radiant and larger than life. Wavy green light is cast and flickering across the lot. Hundreds of old car-park speakers all croaking, peeping, and chirping as on a humid summer night. It's a sonic frog pond pulsating across the wintry abandoned lot.

Samson sits alone in the concession stand, eating Chinese food and watching the light-creatures move across the gigantic outdoor screen.

The small building has been converted into a crash pad and morbid menagerie. Walls are covered with the mounted heads of a taxidermy collection. Wild birds in flight. Bats and albino squirrels. The countertop is littered with Chinese food takeout cartons among the detritus and ephemera of deceased natural history. Bones and stones and rows of mason jars containing embalmed oddities and chemical tinctures.

Sam scoops up some more noodles with his chopsticks, transfixed by the laboratory art film projected onto the big screen outside. Green translucent forms: viruses and spirochetes, twisting, spiraled bacteria, quiver on the screen, cast from undersea, outer space, or between two glass specimen plates. The sound of invisible frogs croaking and chirping over the lot.

Nearby, on the countertop, the vessel of Quicksilver is sitting next to the two milk jugs of orange-colored liquid and a crumpled-up brown paper bag.

Sam sets down his chopsticks and examines the Quicksilver. He turns the vial of liquid metal in his hands. It reflects light spilling around the room from the projector beam and the screen outside. He checks his watch. A late-'80s digital.

- .... .

A slumped and shadowed form, Jonah sits on the side of the dark rural road.

Headlights then illuminate him, as a vehicle pulls up and stops. He's huddled and shaking, shivering in a state of near-hypothermic shock.

We hear the car door open and some heavy music spilling out of it. Sound of the car door shutting again, closing the music inside. Then the sound of a Geiger counter clicking over the idling car engine.

A shadow passes over Jonah, someone crossing through the headlights and approaching. The Geiger counter sweeps over him and he wakes from his stupor, shivering and confused. Then he scrambles to his feet. He falters in the road, struggling to stay afoot, and faces a strange man.

Radiation Man wears a full-bodied radiation protection suit. His breathing is mechanical and regulated. From inside his plastic-windowed hood, he speaks with a voice carried by some distant radio signal, like an astronaut's transmission.

RADIATION MAN
(deep space transmission)
It's cold out here. Get in the car.

-.-. --- -.. .

Jonah and the Radiation Man cruise down the busy freeway in his late-'80s sedan. Instrumental psychedelic road-music is booming on the car stereo. Waves of colored light trickle and stream across Jonah's face as he watches the nightscape rolling by outside the car windows.

The freeway is a future-zone, as if the direction of time is confused. Neon streams of white and red light flow around them, tracers from the headlights and taillights of other cars. The trance music seems to be playing forward and backward at the same time.

Radiation Man speaks a transmission over the music.

RADIATION MAN
(deep space transmission)
It seems as though we are moving forward, toward something.

He points forward, through the windshield.

RADIATION MAN
But actually we are moving backward, away from it.

And then backward with his thumb, over his shoulder.

RADIATION MAN

It is coming. But it has also already happened.
And it is happening all the time now. Like a
giant magnet.

Jonah watches him drive and scans the freeway-scape, colored
light streaming across his own face and the protection hood of
the Radiation Man, like neon tears.

.. ...

Headlights sweep and flood down a row of garage doors as the
sedan pulls up to Jonah's storage unit. Jonah and the Radiation
Man get out of the idling car.

Jonah goes to his unit and unlocks the door. Radiation Man
takes a reading with his Geiger counter. Jonah rolls up his door
and the instrument soars.

Radiation Man enters the storage unit and goes to the word processor. He passes his clicking reader over the typing machine.

RADIATION MAN

Is it in here?

JONAH

Yes.

RADIATION MAN

When you finish it, that will be the end. Where
the words run out.

He exits the storage unit.

JONAH
The end of what?

RADIATION MAN
Go to the castle. Then listen for the sound of
it.

Radiation Man gets back in his ride, cranks up the music, and
rolls away. Jonah watches him go and then pulls his door down,
shutting himself inside.

‑ .... .‑ ‑

Simone stands in the pink hallway outside the office door. The
door is marked *Office*. Defeated, her head hung, hesitating, finally
she musters the courage and knocks.

MR. STEVENS
(from inside his office)
Come in.

She stalls for another brief moment, and then opens the door.
She enters the office and turns, facing the door, as she attentively closes it, disappearing from view as the latch clicks shut.

Office.
A closed door.
And whatever may go on behind it.

Simone sits in a chair before the front edge of the desk, waiting quietly. She pushes her hair back behind her ear, and returns her hands to her lap, nervously picking at her fingernails. Unsure where to hold her gaze, she maintains it somewhere between her lap, the edge of the desk, and the smoke curling off it.

Cigarette smoke curls off the end of the desk like the numen of a sinister presence emanating from beyond our field of view.

The small clammy office is a windowless room of suicidally drab baby blue cinder blocks. Condensation beads and runs down the grooves of mortar between the blocks.

On one wall of the small room there is a standing metal locker, like a sports locker, with a small key in the lock. The cabinet is ticking, from the inside, a thousand tiny little clock ticks. Simone watches the locker, and listens to it ticking.

She attempts to clear her throat as quietly as possible. Mr. Stevens closes an epic black ledger and addresses Simone with expansive and generous tolerance.

MR. STEVENS
Simone, what brings you in here today?

Stevens sprawls behind his desk like an eagle, certain of his indispensable position. There is a classic round school clock behind him on the wall.

The same clock is on the wall behind Simone, so that they are opposite each other, and correspondingly display the opposite time.

                    SIMONE
          (nervously)
Well I wanted to talk with you. Obviously. I,
uh, I feel I've been having a bit of difficulty.
I'm sure you've noticed that. And actually I've
been feeling like maybe I need to take a break.
And so I thought it would be helpful to talk
about it with you.

                    MR. STEVENS
I thought we discussed this already, today.

                    SIMONE
We did.

                    MR. STEVENS
And we agreed that it was perfectly fine for you
to take a short break.

                    SIMONE
Yes.

                    MR. STEVENS
And did you not—?

He finishes his sentence with his hands, waving them in a general magical manner.

                    SIMONE
Yes, I did.

                    MR. STEVENS
And...

(smoking)

…it was not satisfactory?

SIMONE

No. It was fine. It's just that… well… I am struggling, I think, um, personally, I think, to understand…

She has some difficulty continuing. Stevens exhales billowy streams of smoke out his nostrils, puts out his cigarette, and settles in.

MR. STEVENS

Well then we obviously need to examine this, don't we.

SIMONE

I guess so.

MR. STEVENS

I think we do.

SIMONE

Okay.

MR. STEVENS

I'm so glad that you came in to speak with me.

Simone nods, not so sure about it. But Stevens proceeds, interrogating her with seemingly pre-established corporate questions that she already knows the answers to.

MR. STEVENS

Who is responsible for the quality of your break time?

SIMONE

I am.

MR. STEVENS

And who is responsible if your break is not satisfying to you?

SIMONE

I am.

MR. STEVENS

And who is accountable to the person who is responsible for an unsatisfactory break time experience?

SIMONE

Me.

MR. STEVENS

Now. What did you do with your break today?

SIMONE

Well I just took a few minutes to myself just to reflect on—

MR. STEVENS

Exactly. What did you do with your break time, exactly?

                    SIMONE
        Exactly?

                    MR. STEVENS
        Exactly.

                    SIMONE
        Really?

                    MR. STEVENS
        Simone.

                    SIMONE
        I stood in some sunlight with my eyes closed.

Stevens is blank.

He waits for more, blinking.

He does not get more.

                    MR. STEVENS
                    (puzzled)
        Where?

                    SIMONE
        At a window—

Stevens arches his fingers together in front of his face, elbows
on his desk.

                    SIMONE
        In the upper mezzanine.

MR. STEVENS
Like a kitten.

SIMONE
Excuse me?

MR. STEVENS
A baby cat. You stood in a ray of sunshine in
the upper mezzanine with your eyes closed.

SIMONE
Yes.

MR. STEVENS
(relieved)
Why that sounds delightful!

SIMONE
Well it did feel like something that I really
needed.

MR. STEVENS
Of course it did.

SIMONE
But it's so difficult to describe.

MR. STEVENS
No it's not! It's easy! See, we just did it!

SIMONE
No, I mean—the thing.

MR. STEVENS
What thing.

                    SIMONE
            The thing that I need.

Silence, as if some evil has entered. The corner of the room,
a seam of mortar and baby blue cinder blocks. The room is
sweating.

He stares at her. She stares at her lap.

                    MR. STEVENS
            And what thing is that?

                    SIMONE
            Well, that's the thing, I mean, that's the prob-
            lem, because it's not there.

                    MR. STEVENS
            I'm sorry?

                    SIMONE
            It's *like* it's there, like it's *something*, but it's not.

                    MR. STEVENS
            How would you describe it, then? If you were
            able.

                    SIMONE
            I would describe it… as… being either invis-
            ible or not there at all. I would describe it as
            being… gone.

                    MR. STEVENS
            Gone.

SIMONE

Yes.

MR. STEVENS

Invisible.

SIMONE

Yes.

MR. STEVENS

Well then I'm not really sure if—

SIMONE

But it does have a smell.

MR. STEVENS

Oh?

SIMONE

Yes. Definitely.

MR. STEVENS

That's interesting.

SIMONE

I thought so too.

MR. STEVENS

And how would you describe the... odor?

SIMONE

Acrid.

MR. STEVENS

Acrid.

SIMONE

Yes, like something burning.

MR. STEVENS

I know what acrid means.

SIMONE

Yes, of course, well, that's what it smells like.
Like something burning.

MR. STEVENS

Well, Simone, that is, interesting. Burning. Is it
painful?

SIMONE

The smell? No.

MR. STEVENS

Ah, no, of course not. A smell.

SIMONE

Yeah, I would have to say no, not really, except
that then yes, sometimes it can seem very painful and then it is painful, yes.

MR. STEVENS

Simone—

SIMONE

(suddenly urgent)

What is it?

MR. STEVENS

What is what?

SIMONE
What do you think it is?

MR. STEVENS
The smell?

SIMONE
Yes, well, the thing.

MR. STEVENS
I would rather say that you're choosing to make this quite difficult for yourself, aren't you?

SIMONE
How do you mean?

MR. STEVENS
I would rather inquire as to what you intend to do about it as opposed to attempting to discern the nature of a thing which may or may not be invisible and therefore may or may not actually exist and/or smell, acrid, or not.

SIMONE
I would have to find it then, in order to know, how to answer that question, I mean.

MR. STEVENS
Simone—

SIMONE
(crying out)
It won't go away!

MR. STEVENS
(and suddenly roaring)
Simone!

Then low...

MR. STEVENS
(quietly)
You know very well that none of this is
possible.

SIMONE
(also quietly)
But why? I could just quit, and leave.

He smokes, and puts out his cigarette, all in one motion.

MR. STEVENS
Now you see. This is exactly what concerns me
very deeply, Simone. We know very well that to
change our physical circumstances is one thing
but if there's a deeper issue then we need to
be honest about that, don't we, otherwise we're
just putting a little Band-Aid on a much more
serious problem.

SIMONE
Yes. I know. And that's exactly what I would
like to address.

MR. STEVENS
Good. I think that's smart.

SIMONE

But it's scary.

MR. STEVENS

I know it is. That's why we have the structure to rely on. We're all safe here.

She nods.

MR. STEVENS

So why don't you try, one more time, and tell me what it is.

He waits, letting her work it out.

They both wait for it.

SIMONE
(timidly)
I don't know.

And Stevens erupts like a bouquet of spring flowers.

MR. STEVENS

O my dear Simone, of course you don't! Sweetheart, that's nothing to be afraid of. There's nothing more natural in the world!

She laughs, relieved.

MR. STEVENS

But it doesn't matter.

SIMONE

What?

MR. STEVENS

It just doesn't matter. You see— Everything
you're feeling is an illusion. It's just patterns,
patterns and chemicals, coming and going.
It feels like feelings, but it's not. If we stay
focused on the tasks at hand it all works itself
out. We're so much better off when we realize
that there just isn't anywhere else to go. This
is it! Why cause ourselves more headache and
heartache. And, from experience I can tell you,
once you leave the ship you are really out there
in deep space, all alone.

He lets that sink in.

MR. STEVENS

Now. Go take a few more minutes to yourself,
get yourself freshened up, and then let's chan-
nel all that energy into the Event where it really
does matter to everyone.

She nods.

MR. STEVENS

Okay.

She exits the office.

Mr. Stevens lights up a fresh cigarette and spreads his arms the
length of his desk, considering the maintenance of things.

He exhales.

V

Robert's front lawn has been stripped to the bone. One solitary square of sod remains.

Robert emerges from the house and traverses the yard. He throws the remaining section of turf over his shoulder and hauls it inside.

He unloads the last of the sod onto an enormous pile of dirt and grass heaped in the middle of the living room floor. A white foot sticks out from the base of the mound. Robert has buried the mud man.

He hauls a garden hose through the front door into his living room and sprays the mound of sod, watering it liberally. Then he hoses down the rest of the inside of his living room.

He rips the curtains from the living room windows. He grabs a lamp off the coffee table, and swings it like an axe, smashing it powerfully against the table. He roars victoriously, then he picks up the table and hurls it through the front window of the house.

Marveling at his new-found will, Robert rushes back outside. He drags the coffee table out of the front shrubbery and heaves it back at the side of the house.

He marches around the dirt yard like a drum major leading his own parade.

Home again, home again, jiggety jig!
Home again, home again, jiggety jig!

He does a funny little shimmy dance, shaking out all the bugs, and then marches over to the corner of his house. He grabs hold of the corner molding of vinyl siding and rips the corner off his house.

Then Robert proceeds to rip an entire strip of vinyl siding from the front of his house and haul it inside.

.⁻ ⁻. ... .⁻⁻ . .⁻.

Samson rolls along a wide, new four-lane of suburban corporate strip. High halogen lights illuminate the night with a diffuse orange haze and the ice cream truck passes through it like a creamsicle.

The strip runs out and devolves into a service road. Sam rolls his magic wagon over the transition and up the long dirt drive toward an old farmhouse glowing in the night on a rise.

Floodlights illuminate razed earth surrounding the lot. The adjacent fields have been cleared for development. Off-duty bulldozers and backhoes sit facing the house.

And every inch of the farmhouse is covered in white Christmas tree lights, sparkling in the night. Sam parks his truck and hops out.

Bluegrass music is spilling from the house. Samson climbs the front porch steps and opens the front door. Music pours over the threshold.

Samson has walked into the middle of a blistering bluegrass jamboree. Couches and chairs are filled with musicians singing and clapping. Dust rises from the hardwood floor as they stomp out the rhythm.

Guitars, banjos, mandolins, fiddles, washboards, jaw harps, mouth harps, a stand-up bass, and an old clunky piano slide and pick away at the end-of-days Appalachian melody. The furious devil's music fills the living room, melding with the extensive folk art collection hanging from the walls.

Ezekiel Crawfish is a vintage picker with a dirt-farmer's lean and handsome countenance. He sees Sam, sets his guitar aside, and rises to greet his friend. They shake hands warmly, shouting at each other over the loud music.

                    ZEKE
          Howdy, Sam.

                    SAMSON
          Zeke!

                    ZEKE
          How are ya?

SAMSON

Just fine. Just fine. You?

ZEKE

Oh, hanging in here. Smoke?

SAMSON

Nah. Thanks. Don't use 'em. When the wreck-
ing balls coming in?

Zeke lights a cigarette.

ZEKE

Anytime now.

SAMSON

How long you all gonna play?

ZEKE

'Til the fat lady sings!

SAMSON

Well. This should keep you going.

Samson pulls the brown paper bag out of his pocket and hands
it to him.

ZEKE

Oh, we thank you kindly, Sam. Sure does take
the edge off.

SAMSON

Whatever I can do.

> ZEKE

Appreciate it.

There's an awkward pause. The music carries on around them.

> SAMSON

Where's Charlie, Zeke?

> ZEKE

Ah hell, Sam.

> SAMSON

I know. I know how hard this is. But I believe
he's ready.

> ZEKE

Oh he's ready. It's the rest of us.

> SAMSON

Let's round it up. He'll have my hide if I keep
him waiting.

The boys are playing hard and fast on that living room jamboree.

Out behind the house sits an old barn, big and white like a
snowy owl in the night.

The barn doors are slid open and golden straw-colored light
spills over Sam, Zeke, the crowd of musicians, and the large
family household as they enter the barn and gather with their
instruments.

At the center of the barn, a white-haired old man sits in a wheel-
chair in a pool of light. Charlie's eyes are wide and wet. His face
is open, gentle, and afraid.

Sam approaches him and speaks to him privately in a low voice. Charlie nods several times, and Sam backs away.

Charlie pulls a folded piece of paper out of his shirt pocket. He unfolds the paper and raises an artificial larynx device to his throat. He reads his poem in a robotic, electronic voice.

CHARLIE
(robotic voice)

> Men. The land is gone. The land that you dreamed on. The land that was dreaming you. And presently I will take leave too. But my love will not perish. Dear family, sweet music. I love you. Oh how I love you.

CROWD

> We love you too, Charlie.

CHARLIE
(robotic voice)

> All right, you can bring her out now.

From the back of the barn, a white horse is led out and brought to stand in the light behind old Charlie. The horse is stunning, a smooth pearl, a real beauty. She nods and shivers her coat.

Charlie looks to Sam.

CHARLIE
(robotic voice)

> Sam.

Sam steps forward again. He leans over Charlie and rolls up his shirtsleeve. He wraps his arm with rubber tubing. He produces a syringe of Quicksilver. He leans over Charlie again for a moment and then he backs away.

Charlie waits with his head down. He jerks a little. And then he looks up quickly, gazing out, above and beyond the men, his eyes filled with light. He raises the speaking device to his throat again.

> CHARLIE
> (robotic voice)
> It's beautiful.

He nods his head in short quivers as if to say, "Okay, okay, okay." Samson and three other men move to his side and whisper a count. They pick him up and move him to the horse. As gently as they can, they lift Charlie onto the mare while another man holds her by the harness and keeps her calm. They lay Charlie onto her back.

The mare shifts nervously and Charlie strokes her with his hand, his head lying over her shoulder, whispering.

> CHARLIE
> (to the horse, a whisper)
> It's okay.

He cries a little. Then stops suddenly—

Blood pours from Charlie's nose, running profusely down the horse's shoulder, bright red across her ivory coat.

A tone cuts through the barn: The strings of a guitar begin humming and droning, drawn by some current in the air, a fingerless raga throbbing and whining painfully. Then a violin. A stand-up bass. The old boys are playing a country death dirge around the horse in a ring of light in the darkened barn.

Outside, the old white barn glimmers in the blue-black night.

Music swells from the barn. It begins to hammer and beat, dirge infusing with electronica… carrying over the field and the black trees.

.. ...

Samson pilots his white medicine wagon down another country road. The alien beat is in full force now.

A large modern pole-barn sits in the middle of a black field. The building is constructed of translucent, corrugated fiberglass. Techno dance music pounds from inside and an interior light show lights up the building in the field like a strobing cocoon full of fireflies.

Masses of bodies coagulate and swarm around the building in fluid shifting hives and amoeba-like patterns, moshing pods of young teenagers: 12-, 13-, 14-year-olds.

Samson rolls his truck up the long drive leading to the hyper-urban barn. He parks, and kids rush the truck, lining up at the service window. They're all talking and shouting madly in the impossibly animate physical language of monstrous teens and pre-teens.

Sam deals cubes of colorful pills, papers, and plants out of the side of his truck like a taco stand.

A lanky kid, taller than the rest, approaches through the center of the pack. He is lithe and wide-eyed and innocently cocksure, looking out from the herd of beaming animal eyes. Jerry is a heartbreaking combination of boldness and naïveté.

> JERRY
> Hey! Over here! I want the best you got!

> SAMSON
> Everything I got is the best I got. Next.

> JERRY
> Not for me. I want the best. I wanna blow my mind!

> SAMSON
> A blown mind is a mind blown.

> JERRY
> Well that's what I want.

> SAMSON
> Put a helmet on it or there won't be anything to blow. Next.

More kids crowd in.

Jerry seems hurt and annoyed.

> JERRY
> Hey man, I'm talking to you. Don't ignore me. I want something real.

> SAMSON
> Then you've come to the wrong place.

> JERRY
>
> I know what you've got.

Sam tries to ignore this, but Jerry zeroes in.

> JERRY
>
> I said, I know what you've got.

Sam looks at Jerry, looks him in the eyes, and sees that even for a kid he is not kidding around.

> SAMSON
>
> All right, everybody, that's it! Shop's closed, everybody have a good evening!

Sam tries to close up shop but the crowd surges and erupts with discontent.

From overhead, the amassing crowd of kids is swarming and festering like a school of piranha, multiplying in mass, and ultimately covering the truck itself until there is only a shapeless throng of kids.

They flood the interior of the truck and emerge with Samson in their throes. He rides them like he's surfing an out-of-control wave at a punk show. They bring him to the ground and cover him like a posse of wild boars.

Another pod of the adolescent animals pours through the truck, looking for the sought after loot.

> KID
>
> I got it, Jerry! I got it!

> JERRY

Give it to me. Come on.

The kid hands Jerry the vial of mercury. Jerry produces a syringe and takes off his coat. He pulls the cap off the needle.

The crowd calms down and is watching. Samson is standing now, surrounded by a platoon of boys.

> SAMSON

You don't want to do that.

> JERRY

Shut the fuck up.

> SAMSON

You have to listen to me. This is too much.

Jerry marches over to Samson and right-hooks him hard with an open fist across the cheek bone.

> JERRY

Now. Somebody help me out here. Come on.

A couple of boys move around and help him load it up and load it in. He gazes at Sam.

> JERRY

You don't have any idea what we've seen.

Jerry and Samson look each other in the eyes while the boys inject Jerry with mercury. The boys back away and Jerry stands alone rubbing his arm. Then he suddenly jerks back like he got punched in the chest.

JERRY

Holy crap.

He spins his head back and forth like he's shaking something out
of his ears and trying to clear his vision.

Then his fingers start going nuts like overturned insects, twitching and twittering with internal calculations.

JERRY

It's amazing. It's—everything.

But the calculations get more intense.

JERRY

Oh fuck. Oh fuck.

KID

Come on, Jerry, stay with it. You can do it.

SAMSON

It's too late. There's nothing he can do now.

Jerry bears down and concentrates. He slowly brings his rabid
fingers close together so they can communicate. Now it looks
like he's playing a high-speed, multi-digit video game, but there's
no game there.

KID

That's it, Jerry! That's it! He's gonna beat it.
Watch. He gonna beat it.

But the game is too much for him. It overtakes him. He loses
all control over his nerves. He's shaking and kicking and swat-

ting at an invisible swarm of bees. He panics and begins to cry, genuinely terrified, a child again now.

> JERRY
> Ahh! Fuck! Ahh! Get it out of me! Fuck! Somebody help me! It hurts! Please—

> KID
> Do something!

> SAMSON
> I'm sorry.

Then Jerry sees something. He stops, and for a moment he is calm, looking out over the heads of the crowd. Samson looks down, as if to turn away.

> JERRY
> Oh no. It's coming.

Jerry gags, and then retches forward, puking all over the ground a copious amount of silvery liquid.

> JERRY
> What is that?

The ground is covered in little silver fish, dozens of shiny metallic bait fish flipping on the ground, drowning in air. Jerry has puked fish. And he's scared.

> JERRY
> What the fuck is that?!

> KID
> It's fish, Jerry.

Then he gags again, more violently, and a large fish head emerges from his mouth. Retching again, he evacuates a full-grown fish, a good-sized rainbow trout. The trout flops on the ground, glistening with a spectrum of iridescent colors, gills drawing on the cold night and the rave music in the background.

Jerry stares down at his catch in horror and disbelief, twitching with a feverish brokenness. A trickle of blood runs from his nose.

Then he turns and runs, straight out into the black field. He runs. And he falls. And he doesn't get up. Sprawled in the black winter cornfield, on the perimeter of light.

VI

The long pink hallway rolls by. Someone is walking down that hall at a resolute pace. A corner is turned, heading into another lengthy section.

Mr. Stevens sits at his desk doing paperwork and smoking. There's a pounding at the office door and then Samson lets himself in.

> MR. STEVENS
> Come in.

Sam drops the two jugs of orange liquid onto Stevens' desk and flops into a chair.

> MR. STEVENS
> Sam, Sam, the medicine man.

> SAMSON
> No more kids, Jack.

MR. STEVENS
(arid, but sincere)
But I love kids.

SAMSON
No more kids. They're fucking crazy.

MR. STEVENS
Oh what's the difference?

SAMSON
There's a big difference.

MR. STEVENS
They're just kids.

SAMSON
They're fragile, and unpredictable, and bonkers. And you don't give a shit about kids.

MR. STEVENS
(assertively)
The world is over, Sam. But the nice thing about *children* is that there will always be more of them.
And if we don't keep them entertained they will tear us all to pieces.

SAMSON
That's heartwarming.

Stevens takes a drag and starts over.

MR. STEVENS
So what do we have here?

SAMSON
Dimethyltryptamine diluted with a mono-
amine oxidase inhibitor for oral consumption.
Grows just like plain old lawn grass, but it's
extremely potent, and not easy to come by in
this quantity.

MR. STEVENS
Your services are greatly appreciated.

SAMSON
Save it. I'm a free agent. And I won't be held
responsible for your theatrics.

MR. STEVENS
Oh will you relax. It's not actually going to kill
them.

Stevens flicks his eyes at the camera.

SAMSON
You have no idea what it's going to do.

MR. STEVENS
It's *all* been highly scripted.

SAMSON
Once you go down this road the script is use-
less. You're off the map and you're drifting in
very deep water.

MR. STEVENS

That's precisely the idea, Sam, and you know
that as well as I do.

SAMSON

I do not pretend to be someone else's salvation.

Stevens loses his temper.

MR. STEVENS

Then *that's* where you're deluding yourself.
And that's why you're still peddling formalde-
hyde and why you're working for me. So get
off your high horse and enjoy the show. You
made this deal. Don't forget that. Now if you'll
excuse me.

SAMSON

I don't need your firewater, Jack.
Someday you're gonna choke on it.

Sam exits and slams the door. Mr. Stevens lights up another cigarette and returns to his paperwork.

.. ⁻.

Samson passes through a steel door and enters the loading dock
sector on his way out of the building. He walks by garage doors
and open trailers backed up to the docks.

Then he hears a quiet voice, and he stops. He looks toward the
dark, open trailers. A woman's voice is mumbling softly out of
the blackness.

Sam walks over to the dock utility light and turns it on. He pivots the mechanical arm and points it into the trailer. The inside of the trailer contains a few glass racks full of water glasses. He swings the spotlight on its arm.

Simone is huddled up on the floor in the back corner, smoking a cigarette. She holds up a hand to block the light.

> SIMONE
> Who's there?

> SAMSON
> You work here?

> SIMONE
> Yeah.

> SAMSON
> All right, sorry to bother you.

> SIMONE
> Wait. What time is it?

He hesitates.

> SAMSON
> It'll be over soon.

> SIMONE
> How do you know?

Sam looks down and thinks about that.

Then he turns and looks straight into the camera. A bright light shines in his mirrored sunglasses, reflecting the light back into the camera. He peers in closer.

Then he walks away. Simone squints into the light, trying to make sense, smoke from her cigarette curling sculpturally in the harsh beam.

-.-. --- -.. . .-.-.-

In his self-storage unit, Jonah sits at the vinyl-upholstered card table he's using for a desk. His fingers clacking on the plastic keyboard of the bulky typing machine. His breath steaming in the cold, dry air. The bare light bulb. His boots. The metal walls. His brown winter coveralls. His watch tiny ticking. Orange light from the glowing screen illuminates his face as he types in the night.

Outside the storage unit, the horizontal lines of the closed garage door and the clacking sound of his fingers typing on the plastic keyboard.

JONAH

(typing)

If you take the smallest increment of time and split it like an atom, is there a singular moment wherein all things are revealed and all things come to pass? If so then this moment is injected into every moment for all of time's eternity.

Garage doors are lined up like blank faces.

> JONAH
> (typing)
> At the edge of human, there is a strange white noise, the sucking, suckling sound of the universe falling into the emptiness of itself.

A floodlight, illuminating the black winter vapor.

> JONAH
> (typing)
> In a perfectly sterile environment the most lethal of sicknesses is life itself, and we are haunted by the shadows of ourselves.

The typing stops.
Quiet outside.
The wash of faraway traffic.

The long rows of storage units, facing each other.

Inside, the word processor sits on the card table, the screen is glowing, but Jonah lies on his mattress wrapped up in a wool blanket and his sleeping bag. He's shaking and sweating, shivering violently, a fever sweat, a hallucinatory brain-boil.

A flaming glow suddenly illuminates the space, and the cutting sound of a blowtorch. Jonah opens his eyes and his face is aglow in an orange fiery light.

He sits up and looks at the light source. He reaches out his hands to warm them.

A small mushroom cloud is burning away on the concrete floor at the center of the room. The perpetual mushroom cloud fires away like a holographic furnace. Orange, red, green, blue, yellow, white. It's pretty, and warm.

Then it's gone. And he's illuminated by a cold white light. Striations of watery translucence shift across his face.

A large ice cube has replaced the mushroom cloud. At the center of the ice block is a figure, a little boy, frozen with his hands up, and wearing an orange life preserver.

Jonah gets on his feet and approaches the ice block. He runs his own hands along the side of the ice block, looking in at the frozen boy. The ice is flowing with interior strata and delicate crystalline light.

Ice melting and pooling on the floor—

And then there's nothing there, just a pool of water on the floor. The bare light bulb overhead is reflected in the water.

Jonah turns and sees himself lying on the mattress, like a mummy in the sleeping bag. Motionless and frosted dead.

Just outside the door, a loud banging erupts from inside the aluminum garage. Jonah is pounding on the metal door from inside his cell.

> JONAH
> (shouting from inside)
> Sam! Sam, I'm not finished yet. I need more
> time. I've changed my mind, Sam. I need more
> time. I wanna be with people, Sam. Sam! Sam!
> Sam!

He bangs frantically, but no one is there. The alleyway of storage units is empty and indifferent.

- .... .

Out on the dark field, the old lonely tree comes alive, a skeletal form of electric-blue light throbbing and pulsating, strands of energy coursing along its branches, trunk, and root-system buried in the ground. The tree of electric light explodes on and off, short-circuiting. Then the night is black.

.--. .-. --- -... .-.. . --

A glow of light emerges from outside, underneath the crack in the storage unit door. And then two beams of light scanning under the door. An insect enters, crawling under the door, ticking, clicking, probing, and glowing. A glowing, irradiated cockroach.

The cockroach finds its way to the center of the room and takes in its surroundings, scanning, processing, and pulsating with light. The bug glows brighter and brighter, throbbing with light and colors until it is nearly illuminating the entire space in waves of colored light, pulsing and dimming like a luminescent scarab.

Jonah is in a deep fever-sleep bundled up in his sleeping bag on the mattress. The cockroach approaches him, ticking across the floor. Jonah's face radiates in the metallic-colored light of the insect.

The cockroach climbs up onto the mattress, crawls across Jonah's face, and then disappears inside his mouth.

A bundle of light descends down the interior of the sleeping bag, headed toward Jonah's belly. The sleeping bag pulsates momentarily like a glowing cocoon, and then the space is black.

VII

Thousands of houses sprawl into the cold countryside. But the sky is blue now, washing color across the world. Patches of snow and green grass. Newly planted bright-green pine saplings and bright white siding.

Brand new homes, everywhere for everyone.

.-- .. - ....

The long row of storage units lined up bluntly in the clear winter light.

Jonah's door rolls up with a clatter. He emerges and rolls the door back down. His fever broken in the night, he's pale, but alive. He locks the door and walks away.

Halfway down the row, he stops, nursing a thought. He turns around and heads back to the storage unit door. He handles the lock, as if something doesn't add up.

Then he lets it go and continues on his way.

The exterior of Robert's house is wrecked, completely stripped of siding, all exposed plywood and fireproofing like a body without skin. The lawn is stripped of grass, a square crater of dirt butting up to the line of green lawn next door.

The living room is a catastrophe. Robert has land-filled the interior of his living room with the exterior of his house. All the siding from the outside of the house is piled on top of the mound of his lawn, from floor to ceiling.

He sleeps now like an innocent, passed out in his recliner amid the wreckage of last night's work. The television is blasting a blizzard of early morning TV snow. A calm spectacle of post-disaster.

Then an obnoxious tone cuts across the tube, a test signal from the Emergency Broadcast System and Robert stirs awake.

He requires a moment to figure out where in the hell he is, and he marvels dryly at the room, putting the pieces of memory together. Then he shuts off the TV and heads upstairs.

Halfway up the stairs Robert pauses to oversee his creation, and he issues half a smile.

- .... .

Jonah enters the Convention Center and wanders through the vast airport of a complex. He passes through the steel doors of a service entrance and enters the long pink hallway.

Mr. Stevens' office door is ajar. He is sitting at his desk, smoking and doing paperwork. There is a polite knock on the door.

> MR. STEVENS
> (from inside)
> Yes. Come in.

Jonah quietly pushes open the door and enters the small windowless room.

Mr. Stevens does not look up from his desk.

> JONAH
> Excuse me.

> MR. STEVENS
> Yes?

> JONAH
> I've come to apply for a job.

> MR. STEVENS
> (impassively)
> Fantastic. Just have a seat and I'll be right with you.

Jonah takes a seat on a folding metal chair, and waits.

Mr. Stevens shuffles some papers around and puts out his cigarette. He regards Jonah over the top of spectacles he's been wearing to do his bookkeeping.

> MR. STEVENS
> Okay, what do we have here?

Jonah hands him a folded piece of paper. Mr. Stevens unfolds the paper.

> MR. STEVENS
> Land surveyor. Interesting. That seems like a reliable job.

> JONAH
> Yeah, it was.

> MR. STEVENS
> Have you been with us before?

> JONAH
> No, I don't think so.

> MR. STEVENS
> Well what we're doing here is something very special.

> JONAH
> Of course.

> MR. STEVENS
> I'll need to ask you a few questions.

> JONAH
> Okay.

Stevens pulls a clipboard out of a drawer and flips over a few pages.

> MR. STEVENS
> Here we are. What is the nature of the Universe?

JONAH

Excuse me?

MR. STEVENS

I said, what is the nature of the Universe?

JONAH

Um, I was here just to apply for a job as a cater-waiter.

MR. STEVENS

And it says on your resume that you were also a writer. Is this true?

JONAH

Yes.

MR. STEVENS

And so I am asking you, what is the nature of the Universe?

JONAH

Well. I'm not really sure if I'm qualified to—

MR. STEVENS

Let me explain something to you.

He takes off his spectacles and folds them carefully.

MR. STEVENS

Entertain my explanation that as a writer you should already know well. We live our lives in the shadowed rut of the wheel. We spend them, day by day, driveling away, and waiting.

And what on earth are we waiting for? We are waiting to be lifted out of the trenches into a moment of illumination, a moment of clarity and certainty, a moment of direct experience wherein all pain and confusion dissolve, if only for that brief and fleeting moment.

He lights another cigarette.

> MR. STEVENS
> This is what we do *here* at the Event Horizon. We engineer moments. Perfect moments for imperfect people.

He smiles broadly.

> MR. STEVENS
> There are people out there in the world right now, waiting for the Event. Waiting and waiting and waiting. Sitting quietly in the dark. Shivering, terrified and confused like little poodle dogs. Yet each of them is, in their own way and by their very existence, on intimate terms with the nature of the Universe and so I am asking you, a *writer*, in your own words, what is the nature of the Universe?

> JONAH
> I don't know.

> MR. STEVENS
> We appreciate your application. Have a good day.

JONAH

I'm sorry?

MR. STEVENS

I said, have a good day.

Mr. Stevens returns to his paperwork, disregarding Jonah.

Jonah sits there, unsure what to do now. He watches Mr. Stevens working and considers his options. He looks at the door, he looks at Stevens, and he looks over at the metal locker which he has just now noticed is ticking from the inside with a thousand tiny ticks.

JONAH

The problem with cracking the code is that the answer is in code.

Stevens looks up from his ledger and gazes at Jonah quizzically over his spectacles.

MR. STEVENS

Fine. If you like, you can start now, for today's Event. You'll find a tuxedo uniform and make-up in the locker room.

JONAH

Make-up?

MR. STEVENS

Oh yes. There are no spectators here. Everyone's a participant. Go get cleaned up and find a task out in the Main Hall.

                    JONAH

Thank you.

                  MR. STEVENS

Oh and I'm afraid I'll need to ask for your
watch.

                    JONAH

My watch?

He points to Jonah's wrist.

                  MR. STEVENS

Your watch. No watches. Rest assured it will be
in good hands.

                    JONAH

Oh. Okay.

He takes off his watch and hands it to Mr. Stevens.

Jonah exits the office, carefully closing the door. The door very
gently clicks and latches shut.

Stevens places his burning cigarette on the edge of a large and
heavy desktop ashtray, which is, needless to say, full. He crosses
to the metal locker, turns the small metal key and opens it. He
hangs Jonah's watch inside the locker on a metal hook alongside
hundreds of other watches on metal hooks all ticking madly.

Then he abruptly turns and glares at the office door, and the
doorknob.

Outside the office, Jonah is standing in the pink hallway with his hand still on the office doorknob, looking at it, as if he's just pulled it closed in that instant.

Inside the office, Mr. Stevens crosses to the door and places his hand on the *inside* doorknob.

On the outside of the door, Jonah is held there, almost magnetically, for another moment. Then he releases the doorknob and walks away.

Mr. Stevens slowly opens the door, just a crack, *the way it was before Jonah arrived.* Then he sits back down at his desk and smokes, visible through the door, as he was at the beginning of the scene.

-.-. --- -.. .

Jonah enters the corporate crab-colored employee locker room. He walks along the rows of lockers. Unsure which locker to use, he picks one. Inside it, he finds a white tuxedo shirt, black pants, black bow tie, and a black cummerbund.

He peels off his brown construction coveralls and goes to the mirror and sink in his long underwear. He runs hot water and washes his face.

While he's cleaning up, two chatty men enter the locker room.

> SUE
> I will say that it is nice to be in out of the cold.
> And the toast is excellent. Exactly how I like it.

They join him at the bathroom counter, running water and washing their hands in two of the other sinks.

Jonah looks up and sees them in the mirror.

> GUNNER
>
> Morning.

> SUE
>
> Morning.

But Jonah is stunned, unsure how to respond, his face dripping with rinse water.

> SUE
>
> If I had a complaint it would be about the but-ter. They say you can't tell the difference but I say you can. There's a difference.

Gunner and Sue are cleaned up, slicked, shaved, and dressed in tuxedo uniforms. Their faces are covered in white face paint, but as a pair they are unmistakable. They dry their hands and exit the locker room. On his way out Gunner looks back at Jonah.

> GUNNER
>
> It was pretty.

Then he follows Sue out the door.

Jonah is left alone with the mirror, the water faucets at all three sinks running full-blast.

.. ...

The garage door rolls up. Robert emerges from his garage with a folded lawn chair. He's combed and clean-shaven and he wears his best Sunday suit. He walks to the center of his dismantled yard and unfolds the lawn chair. He sits down in the chair in the dirt in front of his demolished house, and he waits.

- .... .- -

Jonah enters the Main Hall of the Convention Center through large steel doors. Cleaned up and ready to go, he wears his new tuxedo uniform. His face is covered in ghostly Kabuki-white face paint. He looks out across the giant hall.

The gigantic room is beautifully set for a grand gala event. Tables are glistening with silverware, sparkling water glasses, crisply sculpted napkins, and numbered centerpieces.

At the center of the hall there is a round stage. And circling the tables, a ring of giant blank movie screens hangs from the ceiling at the perimeter.

Hundreds of waiters are moving through the room with water pitchers, filling glasses with ice water. Others are setting silverware.

The collective sound of clinking ice, glass, and silver tines creates a chaotic symphony of metallic tones and pouring rhythms building through the massive space.

From above, the collective motion of waiters moving around tables produces a cascading pattern of motion and stillness like water flowing around stones in multiple rushes and eddies.

Jonah sees a cart full of salt and pepper shakers. He grabs the cart and pushes it out into the room. He observes the activity of servers at work and then he begins placing pairs of salt and pepper shakers at the center of each table.

MR. STEVENS

Good morning, everyone. Welcome to the Event Horizon.

Mr. Stevens' image appears on each of the screens circling the room, larger than life, in his black bow tie.

The servers stop working and watch the screens.

MR. STEVENS

You all look fantastic. Thanks for all your hard work. We've got a super program and I know we're going to have a great year this morning. Now we've got a few special rules. First and foremost, as always, the best thing to do is—

CROWD OF SERVERS

Do it right the first time!

MR. STEVENS

As always, let's be in the here and now and focus on the task at hand. After all, how can we be here if we're somewhere else?

CROWD OF SERVERS

No watches!

MR. STEVENS

Absolutely no socializing with the Client tonight. Very important. Remember, we're all on stage here, so let's stick to our roles.

CROWD OF SERVERS

No talking!

MR. STEVENS

And the most critical rule of the evening concerns our dessert item.

We're excited to be serving a very exclusive
item but we have an extremely limited sup-
ply. So I'm sorry to say that the dessert item is
strictly off limits to the staff.

CROWD OF SERVERS

No eating!

MR. STEVENS

All right, let's finish up and take a complimen-
tary meal break and then I want everybody
ready to go. Let's stand tall. Let's be alert. And
let's have a great show!

The servers applaud obediently.

Jonah notices Simone, also in Kabuki white-face, applauding up
at the screens.

‾ .... .

A smaller corporate banquet hall is filled with rows of long conference tables where the Event Horizon wait-staff are eating
their pre-shift meal.

White-faced servers are filing through a temporary cafeteria-
style buffet line, serving themselves from aluminum chafing
pans, and sitting at the conference tables, eating.

There's a clock high on the back wall, ticking, like in a school
classroom.

Simone files through the buffet with her plate and cup of coffee. She finds a seat at a table, submerged in the crowd.

Jonah walks down an aisle and takes a seat at the end of another long table. The room bubbles with chatter and the activity of eating, like a turkey farm feedlot.

He sips at his coffee, listening to the overtones of the collective conversation. The room swells around him and begins to sound like the amplified interior of an airplane, wavelengths canceling each other out into a wash of white noise. The sound balloons until it is overwhelming.

His sound-thought is suddenly interrupted by the bleating signal blast of a bullhorn bludgeoning the air from the back of the room.

A service captain in a black vest makes an announcement.

> CAPTAIN
> (through bullhorn)
> Sorry to interrupt. If anyone wants to smoke,
> let's do it now.

The servers stop eating and flood the exit. The room empties. Simone is revealed in the exodus, left behind, sitting a few tables away from Jonah.

She gets up to leave as well but then sees Jonah absorbed in his notebook, scribbling sentences. She stands there watching him, curious about this new person.

She waits for him to look up at her, but he does not. She quietly sits back down and takes another sip of her coffee, stalling, watching him, looking into her coffee cup.

The clock on the back wall is ticking incessantly.

Focused on his book, Jonah reaches blindly for his coffee cup. As he does this Simone summons the courage to address him and she abruptly breaks into the silence of the room—

> SIMONE
> Hi.

—and it scares the crap out of Jonah. He hollers and hurls his coffee. Simone also screams, managing to frighten herself in the sudden eruption.

She catches her breath.

> SIMONE
> Omigod, I'm sorry.

> JONAH
> Jesus, you scared me.

> SIMONE
> I'm so sorry.

> JONAH
> Whew.

> SIMONE
> Sorry.

                    JONAH

No, it's okay. Seems like there's plenty of coffee here.

She laughs out loud, nervously.

                    SIMONE

That's for sure. You're new here.

                    JONAH

Yeah.

                    SIMONE

What are you doing here?

                    JONAH
                  (confused)
Same… thing as everybody else, I guess.

                    SIMONE

Yeah. But I mean how did you wind up here?

                    JONAH

Oh. Um, for work— What do you mean?

                    SIMONE

I mean… This is what you do?

                    JONAH

Oh. No, not really. I just needed a new job.

                    SIMONE

Uh huh.

Awkward, he's not sure what to say. She just looks at him directly and he can barely take it. They sit in that silence for a moment.

                    JONAH
          No smoking for you, huh?

                    SIMONE
          I guess not! Not today!

She laughs again nervously.

                    JONAH
          How long have you been working here?

She bites her lip and looks up at the clock on the wall.

                    JONAH
          No, I meant in general.

Simone nods, comprehending his meaning, but she keeps looking at the clock, as if it were a puzzle that needed to be solved, the adding and subtracting of hours passing silently across her lips.

Jonah watches her, waiting, and then he sits back and watches the clock with her. He bounces his knee absentmindedly, in a second-hand rhythm, and he rubs his left wrist where his watch used to be. He gnaws at his thumbnail and looks up at the ceiling, checking out the fluorescent lights and he scans the room until he sees something that causes him to freeze.

He is momentarily captivated like a deer in the headlights, looking intently across the room, directly into the camera.

The camera slowly pushes toward him.

Simone breaks free of the clock and looks at him and follows his gaze, so that they're both looking into the camera, but she doesn't see anything unusual.

> SIMONE
> What is it?

Jonah puts his finger to his lips, gently indicating for her to be quiet, as if some wild animal were in the room.

She looks back across the room but still sees nothing. She gestures to him...

> SIMONE
> (silently)
> What?!

He delicately points in the direction of the camera, indicating that something is there, and that it can hear them. He silently motions for her to follow his lead. Then he cups his hands around his mouth and initiates a fake conversation as if to cover up a real one.

> JONAH
> (in a loud monotone voice)
> HOW WAS YOUR CATERED LUNCH?

> SIMONE
> (mimicking him)
> TERRIBLE. HOW WAS YOURS?

> JONAH
> MINE WAS VERY EXCELLENT. THANK
> YOU FOR ASKING.

                    SIMONE
WOULD YOU RECOMMEND THIS
PLACE?

                    JONAH
I WILL COME HERE AGAIN AND
AGAIN AND AGAIN AND AGAIN AND
AGAIN…

His voice trails off, simulating a receding echo, and he smiles at
her.

                    SIMONE
You're funny.

                    JONAH
I am?

                    SIMONE
I guess we both look pretty ridiculous.

They're just looking at each other, smiling softly.

                    SIMONE
What are you writing over there?

He puts his hand on the book and fiddles with it.

                    JONAH
Oh it's just a… thing I'm working on. Thing
I'm trying to figure out.

                    SIMONE
What are you trying to figure out?

> JONAH
> (reluctantly)
> Oh…

He gestures in an attempt to beg off the question, but something kicks on, and the sound of the airplane fuselage seeps back into the room. Slowly the room begins to fill up with sonic gas.

Jonah rubs at the back of his neck, suddenly wincing in a bit of neck pain. He stretches his head down, and to the side, trying to stretch it out. Then he holds himself tightly at his left arm and raises his eyes and looks at her.

> JONAH
> Something is happening. And there's nothing
> anyone can do about it.

Just Simone's face. All of a face. She watches him as he continues to speak in his warm Midwestern drawl.

> JONAH
> It's organizing us to build it. Self-organizing. It
> is us, building itself from the inside out. We're
> conspiring to engineer the annihilation of our-
> selves. We can't help it. We're falling.

The sonic vacuum begins to overtake the room, very slowly drowning him out. He's looking down into the book, reading from it.

> JONAH
> The shape of things is the tragedy we impose
> on ourselves in order to understand. The

shape we take in the free-fall. Like the dihedral of migrating birds. A drop of water. Or a wavelength of sound. The atomic mythology of matter is inside us, projecting a map of itself. But the screen is actually blank and we are moths, flaming in the light of the projection, flickering in the frame-rate. On and off. On and off. Faster and faster.

The sound of white noise is traumatically loud, like a jet-turbine blasting through the room.

Simone covers her ears, blocking out the unbearable jet wash.

On one of the tables, on a crisp white tablecloth, is a perfectly arranged table setting: Clean white plate. Shiny fork, knife, spoon. Napkin, coffee cup and saucer. Silent, civilized, horrifying perfection.

Across the room, Simone is screaming at Jonah to stop, but he can't hear her. He's absorbed in his book, reading aloud, inaudibly. The two of them are tiny signals enveloped within a cottony, oceanic distortion. A surreal agitation, their inability to hear each other.

> JONAH
> (barely audible)
> It feels like it's coming soon because it's happening all the time now. And the closer we get to it, the slower it seems, like a wheel moving so fast it appears to be spinning in reverse. There is nothing we can do about it because there is no such thing as time. It all happened so fast, as though it happened in one instant. One instant

stretched into one infinite instant filled with an infinite number of instants—

Jonah looks up and sees her screaming silently—a face of Kabuki white-face horror—and all the deafening sound is suddenly sucked out of the room—

The room is quiet.

Simone slowly lowers her hands from her ears.

And then the cockroach crawls back out of Jonah's mouth and quickly disappears under the table.

Simone shrieks and covers her mouth.

                    JONAH
                  (quickly)
              What?! What was it?!

Horrified, she gets up and leaves the room.

Jonah is left alone, sitting in the silence of the empty conference room.

                .‾ ‾. ... .‾‾ . .‾.

Robert sits in his lawn chair in the front yard. He is asleep, with his head hung back and his mouth open.

A black hearse pulls up and stops quietly in front of the house.

A chauffeur in a black suit gets out of the car. He shuts his door, awakening Robert from his nap, and crosses around the car to the sidewalk.

> CHAUFFEUR
> Mr. Adams?

> ROBERT
> Yes?

> CHAUFFEUR
> It's time for your Last Supper.

The chauffeur opens the passenger side door.

Robert gets up from his chair, walks across the yard, and gets into the car. The chauffeur shuts the door and crosses to the driver side. He gets in and the hearse pulls away.

The lawn chair sits empty on Robert's dirt lawn. For a moment, the chair is just a still-life, sitting in front of the house, in the dirt, in the cold air.

Then a tiny, invading wave of sound, as if bleeding and rising from the exposed ground around the empty lawn chair.

Thousands of tiny voices entering. Human voices with inhuman qualities. A mass of the living and the dead. A shapeless horde, speeding up and slowing down, stacked and parallel. Electronic, insect, and familiar.

People. All of them. And finally stabilizing. A crowd of simultaneous conversations. Just voices, congregating invisibly around the empty lawn chair. The masses.

The Main Hall of the Convention Center is full, filled with guests. 5000 guests moving to their tables and sitting at their places. Tables and people, for as far as the eye can see. The 360-degree ring of video screens deepens the interior landscape, displaying various live mirror images, or a reality-feed of the room and all the guests entering.

Robert moves through the controlled chaos looking for his table. He marvels at the room like a wonderstruck, well-behaved kid in a fantastic, new world. The lights, the ambient music, the screens, the people, the spectacle of it all.

He finds his table, #260, and takes an empty seat. He nods and smiles reservedly at a few fellow guests. He puts his napkin on his lap and examines his polished spoon, inverting his reflection as he turns it in his fingers. He flips his coffee cup right side up for service.

A dark tone fills the air, droning ominously through the event hall. The lights dim and a fiery sunset fades up on the giant screens, a red sun melting into a black and molten sea.

A red spotlight rises on the stage, revealing a large gospel singer in a choir robe. She moans along with the music. A choir echoes mournfully behind her.

A gospel lamentation the fat lady now will sing.

GOSPEL SINGER
(singing)
Hear my prayer, O Good Lord, hear my prayer.
Hear my prayer, to heaven, hear my prayer.

O Good Lord, won't you lead me from this life
of despair and hear my prayer, to heaven, hear
my prayer—

The sun sets.

The spotlight fades.

The hall is dark.

>   GOSPEL SINGER
>   (singing)
>   I woke up beneath a burning sky!

The hall explodes with light. Mushroom clouds ignite across the
screens. The choir launches into a fiery gospel call and response.

>   GOSPEL SINGER
>   I stand upon a ground of fire!

>   CHOIR
>   And death done sown my field.

The crowd claps to the rhythm of the beat. Robert claps along
with his table and the rest of the crowd.

>   GOSPEL SINGER
>   Preacher man come to plant the seed!

>   CHOIR
>   Death done sown my field.

>   GOSPEL SINGER
>   And satisfy my principal need!

CHOIR

Death done sown my field.

Looking down on the hall, round tables are arranged in concentric circles around the circular stage. Circles within circles. The room spins in a carousel of grand spectacle.

CHOIR

Death done sown my field! Death done sown my field! Whoa oh oh oh. Death done sown my field!

The crowd roars!

Then the lights shift and the music changes again. A techno beat pulsates through the hall. Stars fly around the circle of screens and the room is transformed into a giant disco ball.

White-faced waiters file from the wings, carrying service trays. Jonah and Simone branch off to serve plates of food to their respective tables.

Jonah carefully sets his heavy tray down on a tray-stand. He removes shiny silver plate-covers from his stack of meals as he sets them in front of the guests at his table. In his white-face and tuxedo, he's like a cybernetic mime, the thematic mood of the room transforming around him into a virtual space-scape of silver, black, and white light.

The guests dine beneath swirling galaxies, shooting stars, satellites, and New Age music. An orchestration of soothing and peaceful ambience, cosmic weightlessness, and gently clinking glasses, the transcendental comfort of consuming a civilized meal.

At his table, Robert eats his chicken. This chicken is outstanding. This is the best goddamn chicken that Robert has had in years.

He nods enthusiastically at his neighbor.

> ROBERT
> (his mouth full)
> My god, this chicken is delicious. Good, huh?

Simone approaches the table and pours coffee.

> ROBERT
> Oh yes, please. Thank you.

Another seated Guest addresses the table.

> STEWART
> Hello everyone. My name is Stewart. I'm your table liaison and I'd like to welcome everyone. Is this anyone's first Last Supper? Anyone?

A woman, Helen, raises her hand eagerly.

> HELEN
> It's my first time.

> STEWART
> Would you like to share your name with the table?

> HELEN
> Helen.

STEWART

And maybe you'd like to tell us what brings you
here today.

HELEN

Oh gosh. That's a big question.

A meteor whizzes by on a nearby screen.

STEWART

That's okay. It usually is. That's why we're all
here.

HELEN

Well, everything used to be different, didn't it?

GUEST 1

Mm hmm.

She gets affirmations from the table.

GUEST 2

Oh, yes, it did.

HELEN
(assertively)
I mean something has happened. Am I right? I
mean, am I crazy?

GUEST 3

I guess you could say we're all a little crazy,
Helen.

Robert observes them pensively.

HELEN

I can tell you what I remember. It was morning.
I was standing in the kitchen. At the kitchen
window. The one above the sink. I had made
coffee. And I was making toast. I was standing at the kitchen sink and the toast was toast-
ing. And just as I looked out the window the
smell of that fresh toast hit me like a freight
train. It was like, BLAMMO! And there was a
flash of white light that just whited out everything entirely. Just blind-sided me. So if you
can imagine that one minute I'm standing at
my own kitchen sink and in the next moment I
am completely overtaken and blinded by white
light and the smell of fresh toast.

Robert and the table are pretty rapt. Even Simone who had been
pouring coffee is listening intently.

HELEN

But it's the next moment... The flash of light
is gone and my eyes readjust to the daylight.
And I can see everything so *clearly*. Everything.
The wallpaper is gone. The *walls* are gone. The
kitchen is just plumbing and pipes and wires
and all the appliances are like these grotesque
robots that have had their skin peeled off. And
it was like I had x-ray vision! And then I hear
this little clicking sound coming across the lino-
leum and it's a sound I recognize but for some
reason I can't quite place it until I look down
and realize that it was my little dog that had
come clicking his toenails into the kitchen like
normal—of course I know that sound!—but

now he is just this quivering, shivering mass of nerves and tendons and *brains*. And that's just about the limit of it right there, I can tell you, with his disgusting little eyeballs protruding out of his skull sockets. And I wish it were the limit of it. But it's not, because I rush outside to get some air and just vomit all over the front walk. And when I look up, and I'm wiping my mouth off…

As she speaks, thousands of guests at their tables are manipulating food into their mouths with utensils. Underneath the tables, thousands of legs and feet, chaotically arranged, all unique, yet all somehow of the same animal. And from high above, the tables form a pattern of dots arranged in concentric circles.

HELEN

The whole neighborhood has been peeled away. I am seeing everything as this horrendous massiveness of pipes and cables and wires and the frames of houses and all the stuff inside all the damn houses, excuse me, and the *people* in there with all of their guts and everything else inside of them. And I look down at myself, finally, and I am the same way, Jesus God. Like a fat cow in a science diagram or something. And everything within my entire field of vision is sort of moving. Like vibrating. It was like a *feeling* that I could *see*. Just the *parts* of everything *together*. That was the feeling. Like the way that, if you've ever done this, if you look at too many *eggs* all in the same place. Or *swarms of things*. Like… bees!

At her table, the guests are all watching her and listening, entranced if not bemused. She slows down, contemplatively, wringing the story.

> ### HELEN
>
> So I turn to run back inside, as if there's anywhere in the hell to run. Excuse me. And when I get to the front porch, I look back, and everything is normal again. But different. Everything is familiar. But foreign. It's all become the same again, and, somehow, well… *foreign*. I don't know exactly how to explain it. I just don't know how I can trust it anymore. I try. But I just can't. It's like we're all foreigners.

Robert shifts uneasily in his chair.

> ### STEWART
>
> You are a very brave woman, Helen. Welcome. Any other first-timers here tonight?

Stewart looks around the table.

Reluctantly, Robert raises his hand.

> ### STEWART
>
> Welcome.

> ### ROBERT
>
> Thanks. I, uh… My name is Robert. And honestly I don't really have any idea how I got here. I—

He furrows his brow and thinks deeply. His life, his memory, his remorse welling up from his gut and into his throat.

> ROBERT
> Could you pass the butter, please?

He receives the butter.

> ROBERT
> Thank you.

Robert slowly butters his roll.

The table watches and waits for him to say more, but Robert fills the vacuum of expectation by eating his dinner roll, laboriously chewing and swallowing until he is finished and has nothing more to say.

Simone is staring at the floor with her pitcher of coffee hanging at her side. A few tables away, Jonah sees her staring off into downward space, catatonically.

> STEWART
> Well we all have to forgive ourselves, don't we?

> ROBERT
> I suppose so.

> SIMONE
> For what?

The guests at the table all turn to look at Simone.

> STEWART
> I'm sorry?

SIMONE

What do we have to forgive ourselves for?

STEWART

I don't think this is appropriate.

SIMONE

I just want to know what we have to forgive ourselves for.

Stewart looks around the room for some kind of help.

Robert speaks to Simone.

ROBERT

It's okay.

SIMONE

No, it's not okay. Don't you feel that something is really not okay?

ROBERT

Yes, of course, but... there's nothing we can do about that.

HELEN

That's why we're all here, sweetie. Do you want to sit down?

STEWART

Helen!

SERVER 1

What's going on here?

Another server in white-face has approached the table.

> HELEN
> Everything's okay.

> SERVER 2
> Was she interrupting your table?

> STEWART
> Yes, but it's okay now.

> SERVER 3
> It's not okay. Not if she interrupted the Event.

Simone is surrounded by white-faced servers. And more are crowding in. She stares at the table.

> SERVER 4
> Who interrupted the Event?

> SERVER 5
> She did.

He points at Simone.

> SERVER 6
> How could you do that?

> SERVER 7
> You've ruined it.

> SERVER 8
> Why would you intentionally disrupt the expe-
> rience for the guest?

SERVER 9
Because she is *selfish*.

Simone is staring at the table.

The guests are staring at her.

And the lynch mob of servers are staring into the camera.

SIMONE
I don't feel so good. I think I have to go. I'm
sorry. Here's your coffee.

She sets the coffee pot down on the table and leaves.

From a few tables away, Jonah watches her go as she crosses
the room toward an exit, but he is interrupted. The lights in
the room fade to a deep red. A deep wave of sound swells
around him, servers exit the space and the guests are restless
with anticipation.

In a far corner of the hall, a spotlight snaps on, revealing
Mr. Stevens' face, shining and slick, beaming in the light of
show business. He wears a microphone headset and sings a dev-
ilish melody, a cappella.

MR. STEVENS
(singing)
If I had ever been here before I would probably know just what to do. Don't you?

A hushed murmur rolls across the tables as the guests turn in
their seats.

MR. STEVENS
(singing)
If I had ever been here before on another time
around the wheel I would probably know just
how to deal.

(speaking)
Ladies and Gentlemen… Welcome to the Last
Supper.

The spotlight snaps off.

The crowd applauds excessively.

A droning sitar rises from the sound-system. A throbbing, hyp-
notic drumbeat. A stream of waiters flows into the room. They
wear executioner hoods and carry service trays full of shot
glasses. The shot glasses are filled with an orange liquid.

Shot glasses are placed on the tables, one in front of each guest.
Robert regards the tiny dessert with a leery eye.

Storm clouds roll across the screens. Thunder and lightning.

Mr. Stevens appears in another part of the room in a brooding,
stormy light.

MR. STEVENS
Friends, we have a bad habit. And tonight we're
going to break that habit. We have been infused
with a false belief. For centuries we have
accepted an erroneous assumption that when
Adam and Eve ate of the Tree of Knowledge
they were cast out of the Garden, abandoned

by God and expelled from paradise. Well, I simply cannot accept this nefarious claim. I don't believe it!

He walks slowly between the tables, preaching like a post-apocalyptic Willy Wonka. He wears a shiny silver suit.

MR. STEVENS
And I am here to reaffirm what each and every one of you already knows in your hearts. We are home. The Garden is growing right in our own backyard. Divine intelligence is coursing through our veins! The fruit is ours to enjoy! And the mountaintop is where we stand because we *belong* here! So do not be afraid.

A woman is weeping, quietly. He takes her hand.

MR. STEVENS
Now there is one character in the Garden who has been ignored. This ignorance has been a source of agitation for a great many years and by now he's a little more than irritated. To get right down to it, he's just plain mad. He's all tied in a knot and he's been causing some problems. Lying, cheating, thieving. They accuse him. If only he'd just quiet down! Oh yes, he's quite a little trickster. Acting like a fool. Speaking in gibberish and silly rhymes. We can't understand him! He talks like a child! Ah, but if only they had paid attention. If only they had listened.

He puts his hand to his ear and listens.

The audience is rapt and silent.

Mr. Stevens hears a pin drop.

> MR. STEVENS
> Well here I am. Ladies and Gentlemen. Say
> hello to Mr. Snake! Because here I am!

The crowd goes wild.

Mr. Stevens runs to the center of the room and takes the stage,
his silver suit sparkling and glistening in full light.

Applause evolves into a rhythmic clapping. Stevens struts
around the stage, clapping with the people like a rock star. Then
he quiets the crowd again.

> MR. STEVENS
> And who is Mr. Snake? Who is this big bad ser-
> pent and what does he represent? Well. What
> are we all afraid of? Change? Uncertainty?
> Insecurity? Yes. Of course we are. But what are
> we really afraid of *now*? Each other?

He watches them. The room is quiet. All eyes, and rapt bodies.
The space is palpable.

> MR. STEVENS
> (intimately)
> Everything? Are we afraid of... *everything?*

He holds a hand up into the light and searches the air about him
with his eyes.

MR. STEVENS
Are we afraid… of *this*?

He quickly pinches his thumb and index finger into a pin-point as if he's just captured a fly, or whatever *this* is.

He lowers it, to have a look at this invisible piece of the cosmos, and then he releases it, freeing it into the room.

MR. STEVENS
(releasing his breath)
Ahhhhh….

A waiter walks across the stage carrying a small tray and a single shot glass of the orange liquid.

MR. STEVENS
Tonight, I invite you to shed your skin. Break your bad habit. And join each other in a new life. Life is a reflection. Death is the Master, but the Master is only a mirror. Let's stop time, shall we? Let's be free.

He takes the glass of juice from the waiter's tray and raises it to the room.

MR. STEVENS
Tomorrow and tomorrow and tomorrow creeps in this petty pace from day to day to the last syllable of recorded time…

The screens display a 360-degree reflection of the crowd itself, a documentary mirror, a real-time feed of the Event.

Subtitles of the Shakespearian chant run across the bottom of the screens, prompting the audience to join in the group toast.

CROWD

And all our yesterdays have lighted fools the way to dusty death…

Robert reads the words on the screens and joins in.

CROWD

Out, out brief candle! Life's but a walking shadow, a poor player that struts and frets his hour upon the stage and then is heard no more. 'Tis a tale told by an idiot, full of sound and fury, signifying nothing.

Mr. Stevens throws back his glass.

The crowd throws back with him.

Robert swallows his shot.

And he waits for something to happen.

Then his eyes go wide as something rushes up fast within him. It swells and warps sonically, crinkling like thin sheets of metal. It scratches backward across the surface of the record as the fabric of his reality tears itself in half.

Robert lunges forward and claws at the tablecloth. He seizes back in his chair and then goes limp.

.. ⁻.

The pink hallway is packed with servers voraciously consuming shots of orange liquid.

Jonah pushes through the long corridor looking for Simone as the other servers begin dropping to the floor around him.

⁻.⁻. ⁻⁻⁻ ⁻.. . .⁻.⁻.⁻

Mr. Stevens walks across the hall, strolling away from the thousands of moaning, convulsing bodies. He exits the giant room and the steel door slams shut. All is quiet in the hall.

⁻ .... .

The service hallways are lifeless and mute. The industrial kitchen devoid of activity. The bathrooms and locker rooms vacant.

The Convention Center is rudderless and adrift.

.⁻⁻. .⁻. ⁻⁻⁻ ⁻... .⁻.. . ⁻⁻

In the Main Hall, the giant screens display a brilliant field of TV snow, silent and blizzarding with light.

Another steel door creaks open, and slams shut, echoing through the cavernous hall.

Samson stands now on the edge of the quiet spectacle, bright TV snow reflecting in his mirrored sunglasses. He takes them off, marveling at the room.

Hello?

His call echoes through the room and draws no response.

At his table, Robert is heaved back in his chair, chest and belly up, arms limp at his sides, neck hanging back like a dead man, mouth open and wide to whatever might enter from above.

His fingers are twitching slightly, floating just above the floor.

.-- .. - ....

Jonah enters the Loading Dock Sector and stands at the end of the long row of cargo bays.

CRASH... SMASH...

He hears glass shattering in small explosive bursts. He walks down the row of cargo bays until he comes to one lit up by a utility light. He stands and watches, looking into the shipping container backed up to the dock.

SMASH... CRASH...

Simone is inside, at the back of the cargo cavity. She pulls water glasses full of ice from a glass rack and hurls them against the back wall of the trailer. The glass and ice shatter against the wall.

She grabs another glass.

JONAH

Hello?

He startles her and she spins around like a cornered animal in the harsh, bright light.

> SIMONE
> Who's there? Stay away from me.

> JONAH
> It's me. We were talking before.

No recognition.

> JONAH
> You all right?

> SIMONE
> No. I'm sick.

> JONAH
> What's wrong.

> SIMONE
> I don't know.

He doesn't know what to say.

> JONAH
> It's gonna be okay.

> SIMONE
> Stop saying that word. How do you know it's going to be okay? Can you explain *okay*? Can you explain this thing that is coursing through me? Can you? It's burning! All I have is my skin. And it won't leave me alone.

> JONAH
>
> Maybe it doesn't want to be left alone.

He takes a step forward but she warns him ferociously.

> SIMONE
>
> Don't come near me! And stop looking at me.

> JONAH
>
> All right. I'm just going to sit down for a minute. Way over here. We don't have to say anything. But that's what I'm going to do.

He moves away from her and sits down against the wall at the front edge of the trailer. Just him sitting there. He waits and he doesn't look at her and then he listens as she talks. Calmly and methodically, she speaks.

> SIMONE
>
> It comes up inside me and it won't go away. It comes up, like a slow geyser of thick chemicals, and spreads through me. It makes me want something. I want it so much but I don't know what it is. It comes up from the bottom like a small seed, just floating there, and it bleeds around inside, looking for me.

The empty loading dock corridor. Empty trailers. Her shoes on broken glass. Ice cubes. Her hands.

And just Jonah listening.

> SIMONE
>
> And it makes me so sad that I will never figure

out what it is, just enough to let it be, all by itself. And because I want it, it won't go away. It needs me to need it. And want me back. I can feel it moving. I can hear it and I can see it, I can almost touch it, and it is some kind of life. It is beautiful and warm and gentle and it is your friend. And then it turns, when you try and put it away, or when you can't carry it anymore, and it isn't allowed.

The pipes running along the industrial ceiling. The work light. Reflections of light in the smooth, polished concrete.

                    SIMONE
It sinks and settles and lies there moaning like a poison. And then it forms itself against the denial. And lives there like a sick frog in the corner. *Deformed...* Something that's not supposed to be the way that it is. *How is this possible?* That something is not the way that it is supposed to be—?

He waits for her to continue and he does not look at her.

                    JONAH
Maybe it's not you that's sick. Maybe it's everything around you.

                    SIMONE
Then what's the difference? That's just words.

                    JONAH
No, we could do things. Real things. Just simple things. We could go, get coffee, or go to the

movies or walk in the woods and look at birds
or—music—things that, uh—stupid things.
Just real things.

She waits for him to say more, but he does not.

Simone moves forward in the space and lies down, curling up
tightly against his body. He has no choice but to hold her and so
he holds her, just breathing. Their breathing takes on the quality
of two mechanical respirators. She allows herself to be there for
what seems like a long time.

Then she gets up.

> SIMONE
> That sounds really nice. But those things aren't
> possible. I think you might have a fever.

She walks away. He hears her walk down the corridor and open
a loading dock door. Outside is the cold howl of space. He hears
this, listening to her consider it. Then the door slams shut and
the loading dock is quiet. She is gone.

Jonah is alone, sitting on the floor of the trailer in his white-face
and tuxedo uniform.

He hears singing, a strange ethereal choir in the distance, briefly,
and then it fades.

He waits for more. But no sound comes. He gets up and walks
down the loading dock corridor back toward the Event. He exits
through steel doors back into the pink hallway.

─.─. .─. .─ ─.─. ─.─ .. ─. ──.

Jonah stands at the end of the pink hallway. The corridor is packed with bodies, the bodies of cater-waiters lying on the floor in a long pile, huddled, collapsed, and intertwined. The very light hum of voices floats through the hallway.

He moves down the length of the hall, carefully stepping through the mass of tuxedoed, white-faced bodies.

─ .... .

In another section of the labyrinth, Samson walks along a corridor. He rounds a corner and approaches the office at the end of the hall. The office door is ajar and he sees Mr. Stevens sitting at his desk.

Cautiously, Sam stops in the hallway at some distance from the office door. Stevens is doing paperwork and smoking a cigarette, business as usual.

                    SAMSON
          Jack?

Stevens looks up from his paperwork and takes a drag off his cigarette. He speaks to Sam in a tone that is oddly too low and hushed for the distance between them.

                    MR. STEVENS
          It's beautiful, isn't it? It's like church. So unnec-
          essary, but so—

                    SAMSON
          How long have they been out, Jack?

MR. STEVENS

It can be confusing. But it's such good fiction,
isn't it? Otherwise what else is there? The good
news is that if God is finally just a figment of
the imagination, then anyone is free to play
him.

Stevens checks his watch and returns to his paperwork. He
makes an entry in his ledger.

MR. STEVENS
(to himself, notating)
In Girum Imus Nocte Et Consumimur Igni...

Sam walks away.

Stevens takes a thoughtful drag off his cigarette.

-.-. --- -.. .

Sam cruises down a length of pink hallway. He rounds a corner
and nearly slams into a waiter.

SAMSON
Excuse me.

Sam keeps rolling. But the waiter stops. It is Jonah. He watches
Sam walk away and then he stops him.

JONAH
Sam?

Sam stops and turns around.

SAMSON

Yeah?

JONAH

Sam— It's me.

Sam is confused, and then he recognizes Jonah beneath his white-face make-up.

JONAH

I think it's—r-r-really close, Sam. It feels really close now.

Sam watches Jonah. He tries to figure out how it is that they're in the same space at the same time. He looks at his watch.

SAMSON

We're inside it, aren't we.

JONAH

It's much—m-more—than I—expected. It's nice to see you.

SAMSON

You too.

They stand beneath the raw fluorescent lighting. The lighting seems to be getting harsher as their faces begin to wash out. An acid wash. Jonah has great difficulty speaking.

JONAH

I didn't want to die, Sam. But— Thank you. The mirror. It's what I— Everything. Happening. I mean— Whole. Inside. It's— In reverse. I don't know how to— It doesn't talk anymore. I I ccccann't— So b-beau— I I— I— I ddidint—

SAMSON
Jonah.

The lights are almost strobing. Their complexions are deathly. Weeping.

JONAH
I think I have to go to the big room now, Sam.
Thank— Goodbye.

Jonah turns around and walks away leaving Sam standing alone in the pulsating pink hallway. Samson watches him go. Then he turns and exits the hall through an adjacent bathroom door.

.. ...

Sam turns on the tap in the large bathroom and rinses his face. He leans into the sink, his face dripping, and looks into the mirror.

He grabs some paper towels from the dispenser and dries his hands and face, slowly, thoughtfully. He gazes into the large mirror, absently drying his hands. He repeats Mr. Stevens' palindrome to himself...

SAMSON
In Girum Imus Nocte—

He stops, watching. Then he quickly backs away from the sink. And a fish suddenly jumps out of the mirror.

A brilliant, beautiful rainbow trout, radiating with color, leaping horizontally out of the mirror, flipping its tail, spraying silvery droplets of water into the bathroom, and then falling sideways back into the mercurial liquid.

The mirror stills.

Sam waits.

He takes a step closer. And leans in a bit—

An enormous king salmon leaps out of the mirror, swallowing Samson whole and flopping onto the bathroom floor. It lies there, bloated, with its belly full, gills sucking at the air, slapping its tail in silver mucous on the bathroom tile. The fish flips over, attempting to throw itself back into the water, and then it finally hurls itself back into the mirror.

The bathroom is empty and quiet except for the sound of the running faucet.

- .... .- -

Jonah walks down a long pink corridor and exits through steel doors leading to the Main Hall where the screens are aglow with the bright and silent light of television snow.

The 5000 guests are lying facedown on their tables and slumped in their seats. Some have fallen, sprawled out on the floor.

Jonah walks across the hall and stops at the perimeter of the tables. He hears them all breathing. He walks between the tables, walking through the still-life of drooling mouths and rolled eyes.

A slight murmur rises from the tables. The bodies breathe and hum.

The humming swells until all the bodies are moaning in a unified tone. A droning chord fills the room, undertones and overtones, bodies singing a vegetable meditation.

Jonah stands near the center of the room, listening to the collection of tones and Oms vibrating around him. Then suddenly it stops and the room is quiet again.

He approaches a body, Robert. He looks at Robert's pale face. He grabs him by the jowls and moves his limp head back and forth. He presses his fingers to Robert's jugular and takes a pulse. Then Jonah takes his own pulse. His pulse is pounding.

Jonah places his hand on Robert's forehead. Then he opens one of Robert's eyes. And looking into his pupil…

We plunge into Robert's eye, descending through the neural tunnel leading to the visual cortex in Robert's brain. The neural network. Synapses sparking and firing. A new connection is made. A pathway to the brain stem. Descending. A spiraling pathway of information. Symbols, languages, icons, sonic surges, and encoded psychedelic patterns of fractal form. Primitive psychedelia. An aria of mandalas, perpetually unfolding, diffusing, and coalescing their visual narratives.

Forgetting where we were, we continue falling through the elements of mercurial evolution, carcasses, insects, and fossils, the horror and music of the spheres, streams of painted light trickling, sucking into the pool, a primordial womb, direction-less, but expanding with the pressure of sound, expanding until we burst into—

Interstellar space.

The black vacuum. Droplets of silvery amniotic-substance glistening reflectively in the anti-gravitational free-fall.

Moving along the periphery of phenomena. Gaseous masses and coagulations of stardust. Rippling dark matter. The perimeter of a solar system. A planet. Moons. The rings of Saturn. More planets. The familiar monochrome landscape of our moon. Then the Earth. And falling fast into—

A suburban street.

Houses destroy and rebuild themselves in a repeating cycle of self-annihilation and regeneration. The neighborhood crumbles and reconstructs in a looping circuit of collapse and assembly, over and over and over again—

Robert suddenly awakens with a loud guttural cry. He's looking up at Jonah.

> ROBERT
>> It's coming.

Robert looks around the room, panicky, not sure where he is, or what's happening. He sees the thousands of lifeless bodies—

The room suddenly erupts. Thousands of bodies simultaneously come to life, and panic.

Absolute pandemonium. Instant crowd hysteria of people not knowing where they are, trying to get anywhere, climbing over the tables, and each other, running through the aisles.

And as though coming to the rescue of the confused and pan-
icking masses, Mr. Stevens stands above them on stage and pro-
claims rapturously into his headset microphone:

MR. STEVENS
IT'S COMING!! IT'S COMING!!

A beat kicks in on the sound-system and the crowd begins to
spontaneously organize. They move in unison, performing a
choreographed group line-dance ala the Macarena or the Electric
Slide. The simple, physical ecstasy of group participation.

The crowd moves in concentric circles around the stage, dancing to the pop beat, through the aisles, between tables, a floral
mandala of people in the giant space.

Robert moves with the herd, dancing up a furious storm. He
shouts over the music, dancing to save his precious life, sweating
and heaving with ecstatic relief and release, joy.

ROBERT
AHHHHHH!!

Over the heads of the crowd, the video screens are blazing
with white light. Glistening and searing. Sound receding and
dissolving…

Nothing but white light.

Illuminating the audience. Us.

And Jonah's quiet voice.

JONAH
Look around. There are people all around you

now. Was something wrong with the world? Was something strange? If each of us at the core is perfect and free, then nothing is happening, and nothing has ever happened at all.

Nothing but a field of brilliant white light.

VIII

Snow flurries out of the white. Heavy traffic flows over a free-way overpass. A silent river of cars. Exactly as it is. The soft winter sky. Muted and unchanged. Flat and folding clouds. Some aluminum ventilator spinning on a rooftop.

IX

Jonah walks down the long row of identical storage units.

He stops at his space and unlocks it. He rolls up the door and gags, forced backward by something he sees and smells inside. He stands in the alleyway, mouth and nose covered, looking into the unseen space.

Then he enters—

⁻ .... .

The open garage door.
The sound of typing.
Clacking on plastic keys.

It stops.

.⁻ ⁻. ... .⁻⁻ . .⁻.

The mud man steps out of the storage unit—

X

The tree is on fire, burning in the black field.
Roaring out of void. Burning in reverse.
Burning into dusk, into black.

XI

Falling snow, inside the globe.

Flocks of black starlings swoop and dive in swirling patterns of aerial choreography en masse. Bright red cardinals ignite with color against the snowy ground, searching for seeds.

The tree stands at the center of the winter field.

> JONAH
> The killdeer come crying across the fields.
> Limping and crying. Like something hot was
> buried in the ground. Eventually there'll be
> some field left, because it will stop. Or maybe
> it'll just keep on.

Bare winter branches cross, merge, and mingle in random patterns of line and space. A thicketed tapestry of layer upon layer.

Power lines. Radio communication towers. And houses. Thousands of hibernating houses. Brand new homes everywhere for everyone.

A lazy circus song gently bubbles from the sleep. The clumsy melody floats through the empty suburban streets.

.. ...

Samson rounds a corner, steering his white truck. He rolls down the street, trolling for business.

A front door flies open and a child sprints across the lawn. He runs down the street, a lone runner chasing the music.

Suddenly all the front doors fly open and children pour from the houses, running across the lawns. Thousands of children streaming from the houses and flooding the street.

The parade of children follows Samson's truck down the street like the Pied Piper. The bubbling, jubilant, chaotic voices of children, running, jumping, and crowding the street.

The voices of children laughing and chattering.

Then silence.

And just children.

Running, jumping, playing, crowding the street, smiling and laughing silently.

.. ⁻.

⁻.⁻. ⁻⁻⁻ ⁻.. .